WEBS OF TREASON

ANDREW PLATTEN

Dedication

Zenia, Peter, Amber, Cappy, and our chosen family of close friends—thank you for cheering us on, listening to our drama, and being our unwavering support network.

Note to Reader

This novella takes place after the events of "Strands of Time and Magic" and before "Chains of Fear and Fury". It can be enjoyed as a standalone story and read at any time.

This book follows British spelling and grammar conventions, reflecting the author's British heritage.

Thank you for your understanding. Happy reading!

MORDELAND

NORTHERN REGION

Dynos

THE HAC

RAILE

MOBI

Sandrick

YARROW

NUULAN

Matalon

Harding Estate

ROSTAL

QUARTT

SOLARYTH

Troll

Haxley

CAVERN

Plainhand Estate

LANTHE

BACKALAR

RAINBOW ARCHIPELAGO

Chapter One

The thin twine tugged at the finger of Jane's left hand, and her lips twitched into a smile. She fought the urge to let out a sigh of relief.

She sat in darkness, her back against an interior wall adjacent to the Master of the Seal's office. The intruder had crept down the corridor on the opposite side of the partition and opened the door to which her line was attached.

He had not made the faintest sound as he deftly tickled the lock open. She only knew he was there because the line, which passed through the wall via the tiniest of holes, had gone taut. Jane could hardly believe the canny old spymaster's bait had been taken.

The Master of the Seal's role was to manage all the Elect's sensitive communications, but as Ghosthand–his alter ego–he covertly ran the nation's spy network, including Jane's employer, Mage Wickham. Jane belonged to the mage's cadre of assassins.

Ghosthand set the hook perfectly, she thought as she dropped the twine, its job done. She rocked silently into a crouch, her ears straining. Those who knew Tommus Wellcram's secret purpose used his nickname out of fear of his ability to influence matters from afar. Those who did not know the truth called him Ghosthand, believing the moniker came from his role as the Elect's ghostwriter, penning most of the ruler's personal mail. Few from either camp used it within his earshot.

Jane had painstakingly stalked the mysterious traitor who had now entered Tommus's office for three moons, almost catching him twice. She was certain he was one of the Elect's most trusted, but the identity of the traitor within the inner circle remained a mystery. The man uncannily sidestepped every trap, leaving so few traces that Jane was convinced he was a mage. Yet the Council of Magical Law's most sensitive snoopers had screened each member of the Privy Council twice, pronouncing them non-magical.

To flush out the traitor, Tommus had announced to the Privy Council that he was investigating each of them based on a tip contained in a letter locked in his office. There was outrage from all, but when he revealed the nature of the threat, the room fell silent. He promised discretion and sensitivity, vowing to complete his search within the week.

Jane edged silently across the floor, having previously noted each loose board and worn joist that might betray her. She slipped through the open door, across to an alcove, and climbed out of an open window. Avoiding the noisy tiles entirely, she circled the edge of the building, keeping to the solid stonework. Next, she shimmied down an iron waterpipe onto the roof of the small outhouse—the only structure in the private courtyard, a smelly but ideal place to observe whoever emerged from the single doorway into Tommus's office.

Worried the shrewd traitor might detect her while she perched above his path in, she had devised the trick with the twine through the wall. If she were discovered on his way out, it would not matter, as his identity would be known.

The merriment from the Elect's dinner for his Privy Council floated out of a window to her right, but she ignored it. Her prey would have picked the perfect moment to slip away to peek at the fake note Ghosthand had hidden in his desk drawer. Jane's mind inventoried the faces of each member of the Privy Council, eager to match one to whoever slunk back to the party. She was glad they had already ruled out the full council, with its dozens of lords, ladies, and other prominent figures. The smaller group of nine had proven challenging enough.

She lay flat and pulled a black scarf over her face. Only her eyes were visible. The material was laced with herbs to counter the pungent stink from below. She had killed nobility before, on behalf of the Crown, and knew their bowels smelled as bad as those of common folk.

She reached her hideout just in time. A soft glow appeared in the doorway across the yard. She felt a familiar thrill, one common to missions where her skills revealed the answer to a mystery–she would finally discover the spy's identity. With her training, her many hidden weapons tipped with poison, and the fact she could call for the guards in the unlikely event she met her match, Jane felt secure. For so many of her missions, discovery meant death, or at least failure. It was pleasant to have the upper hand for once.

The spy stepped into the square. Jane got her first look at her quarry, and it shocked her to the core. They carried no candle–a soft blue ball of light floated just over their head–and their identity...

It cannot be.

Jane was so surprised she made an uncharacteristic mistake, levering herself up a few inches to improve her view. Her quarry's head turned, and their eyes locked. She tried to pull back but found herself trapped in a pocket of hard air that held her immobile. Her throat filled, thickening with some unseen substance that blocked the scream building within her. She could not breathe. For the first time since completing her training fifteen summers ago, she panicked.

Her quarry strolled over, looking apologetically up at her, seemingly saddened by what was about to happen. Jane tried to throw herself about, yanking at her invisible bonds, but they did not yield an inch. She felt herself begin to sink and looked down. The privy's wooden roof had softened, and her hands and knees had sunk through its surface. In moments, she was down to her wrists, and her knees had passed through entirely, leaving only her thighs visible above the damp shingles.

Jane felt the cedar planking harden again, and the air gripping her released its hold. Her throat was still blocked, and the wood continued to hold her firmly in place. The figure below turned and began walking back towards the Elect's festivities. As they reached the doorway, the privy's structure lit with a whoosh of flame.

Jane smelled nothing, her face encased in whatever was suffocating her. She felt no pain, even as flames licked at her trapped arms and her hair caught fire. The spy had numbed her senses with magic but had done nothing to protect her from the unnaturally hot flames.

Jane lost consciousness before the door closed behind her killer and was dead before the murderer slipped out of the side door, away from the party, a mere thirty strides away. By the time the alarm was raised, she was ash.

Chapter Two

Brylee reached across the table and placed her large hand over Mage Wickham's smaller one.

"That's ghastly, Gil. I'm sorry."

She'd remained close to the mage ever since he helped her escape the fate of many charmers—death at the hands of a more powerful magic wielder. Almost ten summers ago, he had lost a good man named Winter during that calamity. He had not mourned the loss of anyone on his team as deeply since. His assassins led harsh lives, and losses weren't uncommon, but Jane had clearly been special.

"We were so careful," Wickham said, staring into the untouched tankard of ale on the table. "The Privy Council and the common servants were screened for magic. We even had men on the roof guarding against anyone entering the courtyard from above. I thought we had all the angles covered."

"Are you sure she was killed with magic?" Brylee asked.

"I went myself, as soon as I heard. The structure burned too fiercely, and Jane's remains—" He trailed off. He had previously explained the heat had been so intense even her bones were reduced to ash. It had taken far longer than it should to douse the flames.

They sat alone in the back room of The Linger Longer Inn. Brylee owned the establishment and stayed there whenever she visited the nation's capital. Like many, she came to town for the opportunities created by the imminent international trade talks. Brylee knew Wickham hadn't sought her out for comfort; there had been purpose in his stride when he walked in and interrupted her lunch.

"How can I help?" she asked. The mage pulled his hand away, scratched the back of his neck, and cleared his throat.

"I need to impose on you, I'm afraid." He was clearly embarrassed, and Brylee's stomach clenched at the thought of whatever it was that he was about to trouble her with. Fighting at his side a decade ago had been one thing, but now she was married with two children. She nodded for him to continue, knowing it would be difficult to refuse him.

"Tomorrow, the Elect will open the trade talks between senior delegates of Mordeland, Thraeven, Landar, and Nydros. He won't be dissuaded, despite threats against his life, as tensions between nations are dangerously high. He believes resolving the bitter trade disputes will steer us away from possible war, and he is set on that path.

"Ghosthand's men intercepted a message indicating an overseas faction with an interest in escalating conflict plans to assassinate the Elect during negotiations. The assassin is someone very close to the Elect, placed here decades ago, but we still have no idea who it is."

"And you think magic is involved?"

"Well, we didn't think so. As you know, the Elect is terrified of mages. He has this paranoid belief that one of us might try to seize the crown. I'm one of the few with affinity he tolerates. He routinely has his staff and advisors examined and won't allow any mages into his palace, let alone on his Privy Council."

"Aren't there a few mages in his court?" Brylee asked.

"In the larger court, yes. That's why he employs the Court Steward to oversee the wider group of lords and dignitaries. And why he meets them at The Lord's House instead of the palace."

"I heard it was because he despised politics and was a bit lazy."

"Well. Two things can be true at the same time," Wickham replied, coughing awkwardly.

"Where do you need my help?"

"Faith Keeper Teyndric and Jacub Morde's devout sister have badgered the Elect into a ceremonial blessing for the Privy Council and our nation's negotiator ahead of the talks. It will be at sixteenth bell today at the Elect's palace. You and your husband have a far greater ability to detect magical ability than the Council's sensitives. I need you to attend and covertly examine those present. If anyone has magic, they are most likely the assassin we seek."

"What in Ag's name makes you think Jacub Morde will let me attend? A known mage, with no business being there?" Wickham crossed his arms and leaned forward.

"I was hoping to convince you to impersonate a member of the Privy Council, with your, er... special ability."

As she processed his words and his meaning became clear, Brylee realised her jaw had dropped open, and she snapped it shut. She was glad, as the words pressing to come out of it wouldn't have been kind. She pushed her chair back, stood, and picked up her tankard, draining it to buy time to think.

"The Elect is aware that one of his closest advisors is a magical assassin, and you want me to impersonate one of these advisors and use magic?"

"It sounds bad, but there is one person we know we can trust. And she's tall–"

"You want me to impersonate Wise Councillor Dunn?" There were only three women on the Privy Council, and two were petite.

As far as she knew, Brylee was the only mage in this world who could alter her own body—a talent she'd honed to survive in the past—and Gil wanted to exploit that ability.

"She was with me last night," Wickham said, blustering on, hoping to overlook Brylee's anger at being dragged into the situation. "At a function on the other side of the city. She's the one person we know couldn't have killed Jane." Brylee's face scrunched up as her mind raced to piece together Wickham's plan.

"We can't both be there. She'll have to stay away. But people will see me, looking like her, and later mention something about the meeting. How will you explain that? Ghosthand has impersonators lined up for such occasions? A bit of face paint to make it sound believable?"

"No," Wickham replied, standing. "Ghosthand has leverage on her. She'll be told to stay away and not ask any questions, no matter what she hears. You know I'll protect your secret. She won't know your identity. She'll be told another mage changed your face. It's rare, but some can make slight alterations without disfiguring their subject. She'll likely insist she be updated on any information she misses due to assisting the crown."

"And The Master of the Seal, Tommus Wellcram, will ask if we can borrow a frock from her too?"

"Of course not. Any fine woman's clothing will do."

"That might fool every man at the ceremony, but Geo Kant, Wenowar Stonebridge, the Elect's sister, and any female servant will notice the difference."

"Surely—"

"Shut up, Gil, and let me think." Brylee threw herself back into her seat and let out a huge sigh. She had to admit to herself it was a clever idea to get close enough to scan the group for magical assassins. She didn't fear being discovered by the assassin. She had maintained her magical fighting skills with Reni. Her concern was sharing her secret ability to transform her body and being in the Elect's presence given he was a self-confessed mage hater.

"How much do you trust Genifer Dunn? Aside from being able to vouch for her location last night." Wickham looked relieved she seemed to be at least entertaining his idea.

"I barely know her, but Ghosthand trusts her with many sensitive overseas matters of state."

"Do you mean she helps him word his correspondence diplomatically, or that she collaborates on his spying?"

"Both," Wickham replied, a wry grin tugging at his lips. "But let's be clear, Brylee, all of the Elect's inner circle are trusted with confidences and well-screened. Yet it seems one of them has a deadly secret." Brylee caught him glancing at the window, checking the time by the sun's path. He was between a rock and a hard place.

"Here's what I'm willing to do," Brylee said. She owed Wickham, and the idea of the nation being plunged into war appalled her. "For me to impersonate Genifer, I need to get close to her and hear her talk at length. Even then, I'd probably struggle to get her voice right. Have Ghosthand steal an outfit she might wear to such events and some of her perfume. Get me close so I can watch her for a bell or so, and I'll feign a bout of tongue-binder—there's enough of it going around to be credible." She shook her head at the ludicrous plan.

"Thank you, Brylee. I wouldn't ask if it wasn't crucial."

"Just promise me Genifer will never know much about me or my family," Brylee replied. A frightening thought struck her. "Does Tommus Wellcram know about my talent?"

"No!" Wickham exclaimed, raising his hands defensively. "Well, nothing specific about you. I told him I have an impersonator with a nose for spotting charmers in my network."

"And he bought that?"

"I doubt it. But he is as desperate as I am. He will let me have my secrets."

Chapter Three

When Wickham brought Brylee into the Master of the Seal's office disguised as Genifer Dunn, it was one of the rare occasions the spymaster's surprise showed on his face. His piercing blue eyes locked onto her as she entered, his cold, calculating, angular features pinched in puzzlement. He drew himself to his feet, rising five inches taller than Brylee's imposing five-foot-ten, then strode purposefully around to take her hand.

"Wise Councillor Dunn. You look very much like yourself," he said as he took in every last detail.

It had been a stroke of luck that Dunn was scheduled to meet her seamstress that day. Brylee posed as Wickham's niece and locked herself into one of the changing rooms while he waited in the shopfront, acting appropriately bored as he sat in the seats provided. At their request, the assistant brought her a dozen outfits, which Brylee insisted on trying in private. It was a simple matter to magically craft a peephole to spy on Dunn when she arrived, and the mirror in her changing room let her check that the changes she wrought on herself matched perfectly. Brylee bought an identical dress to Genifer's, but Wickham wouldn't say where he obtained the jewellery and perfume.

Brylee tapped her throat in reply.

"She can't replicate the voice and all facial expressions in such a short time," Wickham said, explaining the tongue-binder ruse. Tommus walked around Brylee, making no attempt to hide the fact he was studying her intently. He projected a menace that dominated the room; every gesture, every twitch of his fingers, was precise, as if every movement was part of a strategy only he could see. His silver hair might soften other men's appearances, but combined with his sharp, chiselled jawline and high cheekbones, it only enhanced Ghosthand's look of ruthless cunning, which terrified Brylee.

She scanned his link to the source of magic, examining it in detail from his body to where it touched the world's timeline and mingled with the millions of others from living things. Unlike the man himself, his link was unremarkable. Non-magical, she was certain.

Most mages could see the aura that naether—the lifeforce from the gods—created in a person as they consumed it to live. They could distinguish between the non-magical, charmers, and mages of great power. A small fraction, mostly healers, had the ability to see the beginning of the link to the source, though many knew it existed. This was the connection a predator would tear from their victim to steal their power, leaving them to die. Brylee only knew a handful of mages who could follow the link to its terminus. Wickham was aware of the full extent of the link in theory, yet had long struggled to see it all.

"I've already waylaid the real Genifer; she won't be attending. Would you recognise the members of the Elect's council?" Tommus asked. "I can't introduce you, as Genifer knows them already."

"Gil has described them. I think so." The sight of Genifer Dunn's image speaking with Brylee's voice clearly unsettled Tommus, and he stepped back behind his desk.

"Then we had better go," he said, picking up a file. "Let's get you settled before the others arrive. I'll explain your illness and ensure they leave you alone. If our Faith Keeper doesn't blather on too much, this should be over quickly. Will you wait for us here, Wickham?" The mage nodded.

Through Wickham, Brylee had learnt that the Elect was privately apathetic towards religion. Yet one wouldn't know it from his private chapel. It matched the Church of Ag's cathedral for splendour, despite its small size.

Two massive chandeliers, carrying dozens of candles each, hung on golden chains from the high, coffered ceiling. Above, religious figures were painted in rich detail, their forms familiar, though Brylee wasn't church-wise enough to name them.

Thick, eight-inch oak floorboards ran lengthways up the oblong room. Motes of dust settled in coloured beams of light streaming through ornate, arched windows, which lined the left side of the space. They had entered at the front of the room, which was arranged with two groups of seating. On Brylee's right were individual chairs for the Elect and his family, and to her left were four rows of carved benches with burgundy cushions for others. She estimated that perhaps thirty of the most important rumps in the nation could fill the seating, with room for maybe a dozen people standing at the rear.

"Sit in the back row," Tommus said, marching ahead. "The chapel won't be full today. I'll suggest they leave an empty row ahead of you to avoid catching your infection. Wenowar won't be happy, though–she likes the back row so she can doze without attracting attention."

Brylee walked to the seat Tommus pointed to but froze when she saw the altar and the surrounding area. There was more wealth there than she'd ever seen in one place. There was no pulpit, just a raised dais, a solid carved table covered in chalices, candlesticks, and a stand from which a beautiful censer hung on silver chains, belching incense. The wall behind was covered by a tapestry adorned with symbols she recognised from the Church of Ag, though there were nods to other religions as well. She hadn't taken it all in when the members of the Privy Council entered, interrupting her inspection.

True to his word, Tommus intercepted them and explained 'Genifer's predicament,' earning her sympathetic looks, nods, and friendly waves as the Elect's government took their seats. The eldest by far, a petite but sturdy woman with blue eyes and white, short-cropped hair, eyed the back row jealously as she approached.

"You poor thing," she said. Once again, Brylee felt weighed, judged, and valued. Vault Keeper Wenowar Stonebridge, the Elect's treasurer, was revered for her fiscal policy and her ability to assess value in all its forms. It felt like the old woman was adjusting a secret 'Genifer Ledger,' downgrading it due to the infection, assessing if some advantage could be taken, and applying a penalty for being repelled from the back row and her nap. As Brylee raised her hand to her throat and nodded her thanks, her magical sight gave the woman's link an equally thorough accounting–normal.

Geo Kant, Principal Secretary and Head of The Trilogy, Court Steward Cutter, and Wise Councillor d'Astor settled into the front row. Sim Glay, muscular and broad-shouldered in his formal Master at Arms uniform, walked over to stand behind the Elect's chair, forgoing a seat. The Elect's wife and sister entered, greeted the others, who bobbed up and down to bow and curtsy, reminding Brylee to do the same. All had unremarkable links to the source, though she found the sheer charisma of these well-groomed people intimidating. She forced herself not to fidget.

A modestly dressed man entered, and Brylee was sure Wickham's rushed briefing hadn't included him. Lean and hunched with age, his long, narrow face was wrinkled, his chin pointed. Weathered yet wise, he carried a quiet dignity that suggested a sharp mind, honed by years of service to the crown. He was accompanied by two women, one near his age and another perhaps half that.

Brylee initially guessed they were family, but after watching them for a moment, she changed her mind. *The head of the palace housekeeping, and perhaps the cook?* She examined their links and confirmed both women were non-magical. She could not say the same for the man; he was a charmer–just barely–but he drew a little more naether than necessary to live.

Brylee could see how the Council's sensitives had missed this man's magic. Most sensitives can't see much of the link itself, so they identify charmers by their inability to control their aura. But this man's glow appeared normal, just as one would expect from someone without magical ability. It was the size and texture of his link at the source that revealed his true nature to Brylee.

Everyone stood again as the Elect walked in with Faith Keeper Teyndric. The head of the nation's religious matters was tall, of average build, and slightly frail with age. His soft oval face had gentle, sage-like features. He carried himself with a wise, quiet authority, but Brylee sensed a hint of vulnerability behind his steady eyes. His link was normal. If he had any personal connection to the gods, there was no sign of it.

Brylee's gaze, both physical and magical, locked onto the Elect, and her mind froze. Slowly, she began to process what she was seeing as the man walked to his seat, ignoring the gathering, lost in thought. Realisation hit her. Perhaps Mordeland's leader went to such lengths to avoid mages was because he was a charmer—and a strong one.

Chapter Four

Brylee decided Faith Keeper Teyndric was far too fond of his own voice. His tendency to stray into unrelated topics was especially annoying, as she desperately wanted to escape her predicament but was forced to sit in apprehensive silence. It didn't help that her husband's intimate knowledge of the real Ag, from his days as a time weaver, had revealed the deity wasn't what the people of this world believed. But still, "Ag, please bless the talks," would have sufficed, maybe with an added, "and avoiding war would be great." for clarity.

After some pointed coughing on the Elect's behalf, the head of religious matters meandered to a halt and the group stood before he could find a second wind. Everyone waited for the Elect to depart, but he had other ideas. He began to walk towards Brylee then realised he was detaining his councillors and waved them away distractedly. As they filed out, Brylee studied him, willing him to turn and leave.

Jacub Morde was imposing—taller even than Brylee by an inch—and had a commanding presence. His pale complexion bore a sardonic expression—disdainful, cynical, perhaps mocking, yet with a hint of grim humour. His head tilted back, his eyes narrowed, and his half-smile curved upward, but his blue eyes remained devoid of amusement. She had only seen him once before, from afar. Up close, he radiated both charisma and intimidation.

"Don't get too near, sir," Tommus said, holding out an arm from his end of the pew as if to intercept the Elect. "Your Wise Councillor has a bad case of tongue-binder. It wouldn't do for you to catch it on the eve of trade talks."

"Damn it, woman," Jacub said, stopping mid-stride. "How did you manage that at a time like this? You're my Wise Councillor of Foreign Affairs. I need you at the dinner with the leaders of the attending countries tonight." Brylee winced, relieved she had an excuse not to speak. She croaked out something that sounded like "sorry, sir"—had a dog barked it—and offered an apologetic shrug.

"See my healer! At once," Jacub said, spinning on his heel. Sim Glay, who had waited politely out of earshot by the Elect's chair, fell in behind his charge as they marched towards the doorway. As they approached, the sound of a commotion filtered in from the corridor. With two long strides, Sim stepped past the Elect, drew his blade, and stood ready to fulfil his oath of protection. The swish of steel on leather as his sword came free was joined by a scream from outside.

"Hold fast, sir," Sim said, reaching out with his empty hand and slamming the thick chapel door shut. He threw the short bolt across, then, deeming it insufficient, sheathed his sword and motioned for Tommus to help him drag a pew across to barricade the entrance.

To his credit, the Elect didn't appear scared. Instead, he reached up and drew an ornate blade from a pair of crossed swords beside the tapestry, tested its sharpness with his thumb, and checked its balance with two practice swings. Brylee took a step toward the sword's twin, then realised she wasn't supposed to be the farm girl from Haxley–the girl who had learned to fight. She was supposed to be an elegant councillor. She would rely on her magical arsenal if it came to it.

She tried her best to appear scared, which didn't take much imagination under the circumstances. Then it hit her–she had no idea how the real Genifer would react. She squeezed her eyes shut, cursing Wickham for putting her in this predicament.

Several minutes passed before a heavy hand pounded twice on the door. Sim exchanged words with a soldier on the other side of the thick wood. Then, with a shove of his hip, he pushed the pew aside, unlocked the door, and cracked it open. After peering out, he opened it wider, allowing a thickset soldier to step partway in.

"We are still sorting things out," the soldier began, "but I must report that Loral Teyndric is dead, sir. The archway at the end of the corridor collapsed on him and the two guards stationed there. They were also killed in the collapse. If you would remain here until we've removed the bodies, it might be best."

"No one touch anything until I've had time to thoroughly examine things," Tommus interjected. "Is it safe for the Elect to pass? Do we need an engineer to examine the site?"

"It may be best, but we've tested it with sword and spear, and it appears stable at present."

"I'll not wait here," Jacub said. "Is my sister or anyone else injured?"

"No one else was hurt, sir, but I'd say your sister is in shock."

"She and Loral were very close. She'll be devastated. I must go to her. Who were the guards? Tivel and Graem, wasn't it? I wasn't paying full attention when I entered."

"You're right, sir. They'll be pleased you remembered," the solider replied.

"Tivel was a loner, but Graem, he had a family, didn't he? His daughter just presented him with a grandson. He was rightly proud, as I recall." Brylee felt herself adjusting her assessment of the man, surprised by his interest in his underlings. In her experience, it was rare for a man in power to pay such attention. The Elect pushed through the door, trailed closely by his soldiers. He called back over his shoulder, reminding her that he expected her to attend tonight, and she had better be healthy.

"Would you be willing to examine the site?" Tommus asked once they were alone. "If you'd rather not, I'll understand."

"I'm not squeamish. Do you suspect something?"

"Acute paranoia is part of my mandate. The Elect typically leaves first. The only reason the Faith Keeper died is Jacub stopped to talk to you."

The Master of the Seal's cold assessment caused Brylee to swallow hard. She nodded, then followed him out. She imagined it would be out of character for Genifer Dunn to physically examine the bodies as Brylee, the trained healer, would. So, she hung back as Tommus knelt by Loral Teyndric in the rubble. Even from a distance, the damage to the bodies was graphic. She allowed her hands to cover her face, not needing to feign horror as she reached out with her magical sight. It didn't take long to understand what had happened.

"Come, my dear, let me help you across the uneven ground," Tommus said after a few minutes. Brylee took his offered hand and allowed herself to be led away, back to his private office. Wickham sat in the visitor's chair, clearly bored, but became animated when they entered and shared the tragic news.

"It was no accident," Brylee said firmly, not waiting to be asked her opinion. When they stared back at her, she explained. "The mortar holding the stonework together is very different from the rest of the wall. I thought it might be a poor repair job, but I'm convinced it was deliberately weakened by a mage."

"What makes you so sure?" Tommus asked. His lips were pursed, his brows raised in skepticism.

"The two guards. I'm trained as a healer. If you have their bodies examined by an expert, you'll find their injuries are unusual. Before the rocks fell on them, they were both struck by a flat, heavy object. The fallen stonework was round and jagged-it doesn't match their wounds."

"You think they were clubbed first, then the rubble pulled down on them?" Wickham asked.

"Not with a regular club, no," Brylee replied. "They would have seen someone with a weapon approaching, and there were no defensive injuries. I would guess someone killed them with a club of hard air, then held them upright as if still standing at their post.

After that, the arch was brought down on them and the Faith Keeper, hiding their initial injuries."

"Wait here," Tommus commanded, and left the room, not bothering to see if they objected. He returned moments later. "I've sent a man to confirm the real Genifer remained in her office, as I'd instructed her."

They discussed matters for a few minutes until there was a tap on the door. Tommus accepted a note from the messenger, who looked relieved to be dismissed and left quickly.

"Councillor Dunn was writing correspondence up until the time of the service, and after handing it off to her secretary, returned to her office and remained there until my man arrived moments ago. On my instruction, he told her of the tragedy and insisted she behave as if she had been present at the chapel."

"You had a chance to examine the Privy Council?" Wickham asked Brylee. She rubbed her eyes with the heels of her hands and turned away. It troubled her to expose the modestly dressed man as a charmer. She had lived in fear of discovery for her first twenty-three summers. Naming him now would upend his life. He probably didn't even know he had an affinity for magic. And the idea of accusing the Elect? That felt like a terrible idea.

"You've seen something," Tommus declared.

He misses nothing, Brylee reminded herself.

"Aside from me, no one in the room had enough access to magic to raze the outhouse to the ground, kill the chapel guards, or hold them while pulling down the roof from forty strides away."

"But you know something," Tommus insisted.

"I know everyone in that room saw the Elect remain behind. Why would they risk killing the Faith Keeper after that?"

"Maybe they had already killed the guards before the Elect decided to linger. They needed to disguise their actions." The Master of the Seal stepped closer, his gaze so intense as he studied her that she was reminded of her father pinning bugs to felt boards. Brylee despised bullies in general, and anyone who tried to intimidate her, especially. She drew herself up to her full height as she squared off with him.

"Before I came into my full power, I was a charmer. I know what it's like to live with the fear and the stigma, and I'll not name another if I believe them innocent."

"I have no interest in persecuting charmers, I can assure you," Tommus huffed. Then, pressing further, he added, "Did you come into your power by skriking another?"

Brylee's nostrils flared, and she stepped towards him, her hands on her hips.

"No, Tommus," Wickham interjected in a voice intended to de-escalate matters. "A gift from a dying mage. You've heard of such, I'm sure."

The Master of the Seal tilted his head, as if considering.

"Brylee, I understand your reluctance to reveal something like that," Wickham said. "You don't know Tommus as I do. Trust me, if you can't trust him." Brylee tore her eyes away from Ghosthand and looked at her longtime friend. "We're talking about the Elect's life. No one cares about charmers who have no part in things. Tommus has many people with affinity in his network, and he has never leveraged it or done them harm."

Brylee stepped away, walked over to the wall, and leaned against it. She let out a long breath, sifting through her options. After a glance at the mage, she turned back to Tommus.

"Who is the man in plain clothes who sat with the two women? None of the three were part of your briefing. He had a long, narrow, deeply lined face with a pointed chin. He was lean, hunched with age. Likely the lowliest man in attendance, yet he carried himself with the most dignity. Humble and deferential, but when the woman screamed, he rushed back to block access to the chapel with his body, protecting the Elect until Glay closed the door. Aside from Glay, no one else acted to protect the crown."

"Bernart Maybone. The King's Stool. What of him?" Tommus replied.

"King's Stool?" Brylee asked, raising an eyebrow.

"Bernart's official title. The modern term is Head Valet, or Master of the Chamber, but Bernart insists on the old ways and Jacub humours him. Centuries ago, it referred to the personal valet who ensured the Elect's private needs were met, including keeping his privy–his stool–clean and fragrant. There was pride in such service. Bernart's a charmer?"

"He is. Barely. I doubt he's even aware of it. He certainly doesn't have the power to cause these deaths in the palace. It's understandable that his power was missed during your screening. You need a specific talent, which few have."

"And he is even more loyal to Jacub than Sim Glay. I agree-we should look elsewhere for our assassin. Anyone else?"

"No. Just him." The lie came easily to Brylee. She certainly wouldn't dare expose the Elect; who knew what chaos that could cause.

"Good," Tommus said as he walked to a side table and poured three glasses of wine from a plain decanter, lost in thought as he worked. Absently, he passed them each a drink, then sipped at his own. After a few minutes, he focused and turned to Brylee.

"What are your plans for the next few days?" Tommus asked.

"I'll return to my meetings with the foreign delegations. I'm promoting contracts for my family's Wispy Weed business. This has been enough excitement for a mother of two." Her heart sank as Tommus shook his head.

"I'm afraid I need to impose upon you for a few more days. The assassin is determined—and magical. You've impressed me with your observations, your analysis of the attendees and the crime scene, and your courage. I want you to continue impersonating Genifer Dunn. She will be at the Elect's side for the next few days, and I can think of no better way to ensure he survives the week."

Chapter Five

Brylee wasn't sure why she agreed in the end, though the arguments had been fierce. It certainly wasn't because the Master of the Seal threatened to issue an official order to force her cooperation; she'd laughed in his face at that.

Poor Wickham—he nearly died of embarrassment.

That the Elect's life was in danger hadn't moved her much. She had never had much to do with him, and by all accounts, he was a bit of an ass—though her brief interactions had shown a different side of him. Why should she risk her life for a man with hundreds of people protecting him? But the fact that four good people had died, one of whom meant something to Wickham, weighed heavily on her decision. And a newfound pride in her nation, along with offence at the idea that someone wished the country harm. She eventually acquiesced to protect the two charmers involved as her experiences caused her to identify with them the most. Either way, she agreed after some handwringing and negotiation.

"Fine, I'll do it-on one condition," Brylee said. "You use your influence to ensure I get good Wispy Weed contracts. Fair terms, mind you, which I would have obtained in the negotiations I'll miss."

"Maybe I've picked the wrong woman," Tommus replied. "For the next few days, you'll impersonate the Elect's Wise Councillor for Foreign Affairs in the trade talks. You'll have far more influence than I do in such matters." Her stubborn objections to being roped into his clandestine plan had riled him greatly, and he stormed out of his office to cool down before he said something that would undo his victory in securing her future involvement.

While waiting for Ghosthand to return, Brylee's mind raced with ideas on how to best pull off the deception. She knew little about court politics or foreign affairs. She didn't even know her way around the palace, though the talks would be held at The Lord's House—the official seat of government—which she was somewhat familiar with from her own business dealings.

"We'll have to take Genifer fully into our confidence," Brylee said to Wickham. He sat in the chair, deep in thought on the same issue. He shook his head, and for a moment, she thought he'd come up with a better idea.

"It's so distracting. You look exactly like her, yet we're talking about her in the third person, but in your voice. But yes, you'll need her knowledge to even get started. To begin with, which of the delegates has she met before? But she doesn't have to know how closely you impersonate her. We could get you in the same room as her, with a screen between you."

"No, that won't be enough. I need to move like her. Walk like her. Sit like her. We need to be side by side, with you coaching me on any differences."

Tommus returned with a tray of food and a better temper. The three of them made and discarded many plans over the next two bells. When they finally had the bones of a plan, Wickham left to send word to Levi in Haxley. There wasn't time for Levi to travel here and assist; it would all be over by the time the mage's correspondence arrived. He would be beside himself with worry, but informing him made Brylee feel better. She dreaded their inevitable conversation about it.

Tommus was certain he could coerce Genifer into participating. She was deeply loyal to Jacub Morde and would want him protected, and the Master of the Seal's leverage over her would ensure her silence. With some trepidation, Brylee allowed Tommus to lead her through the palace to Genifer's private office, her hood pulled up to hide her appearance. She stepped inside, revealed her likeness, and together they explained their plan. Arguments erupted. Genifer didn't fully buy into their explanation that Brylee's likeness was due to the work of a canny mage.

The only productive thing about the next bell was that Brylee heard enough of Genifer's voice to begin to mimic it. In past adventures, she'd practised altering her throat to match pitch and tone, imitating friends and family. It was far from perfect, but the remnants of tongue-binder would explain the difference. Eventually, Tommus had his way, and Wise Councillor Dunn capitulated.

"I'm sorry for all the deception, Genifer," Tommus said. "This is a deadly situation, and we need to act. We haven't done very well so far. Stop fighting us and help."

Brylee had spent two bells studying the woman's expressions. The confusion, affront at not being fully trusted, and anger at being used were understandable. But there was fear there, too. *Maybe that is the key.*

"Miss Dunn," she said gently. "You are right to be fearful. There is a stone-cold killer on the loose. Help me take your place, and you can stay safely in your room." Genifer's tension lifted a little at that, though her agitation remained. It wasn't until Tommus swore to keep her fully informed and promised to intercede with the Elect on her behalf when her role was revealed that she finally relented.

Brylee was amazed at how fast the woman changed course. Once her mind was set on helping, Genifer became all business, full of great ideas. But with dinner approaching, there wasn't time to teach Brylee much.

"The seating has been arranged, and luckily, I'm stuck between Darran Pyke of Thraeven and Seth Na'var of Nydros," Genifer said. "I chose them as I know them least and want to build bridges before negotiations get underway. We've never met, and while they speak our language, neither is fluent. You won't need to say much."

The next bell seemed endless as Genifer reeled off information and tested Brylee to ensure she retained it. Yet it also flew by, with the time to leave for dinner pressing closer.

"Here," Genifer said, standing and opening a tall cupboard behind her desk. She pulled out an evening gown and some jewellery. "This is the outfit I chose for tonight. I don't know how you already have one of my dresses, but it wouldn't do for me... you to show up dressed in the same outfit for dinner that you wore for chapel." Brylee thanked her and stepped into a small side room to change.

"What do I call you?" Genifer asked through the door. Before she could reply, she heard Tommus explain her name was Maud. Brylee didn't hate it, but it conjured an image of an old aunt. It was too late to change it now.

"How do I look?" Brylee asked, doing her best impersonation of Genifer's voice as she stepped back into the room. Genifer stood and circled her double.

"I think I hold my left arm slightly stiffly because of an old injury. I always hold my purse in my left hand, never my right, so I'm ready to greet people with a handshake. And I always keep my hair tied back–I hate it falling across my face." She rattled off several more self-observations, including shaking hands as the Thraeven people did and demonstrating the polite double-kiss to the right cheek, a custom in Landar. Finally, Genifer had Brylee repeat the names and titles of the foreign attendees until her pronunciation was correct in the dialect of each nation.

"Tomorrow, we have official meetings," Genifer explained. "I suggest we rise early. You have a lot to learn if you are to avoid harming trade with the four most powerful nations in the world, or worse, ignorantly sparking a war."

Brylee thanked Genifer, then followed Tommus along a maze of corridors until they emerged into a majestic dining room. As they entered, the chief steward proclaimed their formal titles and names in a loud, deep voice. Brylee did her best to ignore the grandeur and shockingly expensive splendour, as well as more cutlery per seat than she thought possible. Instead, she carefully scanned every person present for magical ability. Aside from Jacub Morde, she was relieved to find she was the only person with power present.

The Elect was speaking to a tall woman in long, papaya-coloured robes of state. Hearing the steward's announcement, he led her across by the elbow and introduced her to Tommus. Brylee noticed the woman's hand lingered on Jacub Morde's elbow a fraction longer than necessary–and that he noticed it, too. His smile suggested there was a closeness between them. *More than a friendship?*

"Caelon Black, Prime of Landar, I'd like you to meet Tommus Wellcram, Mordeland's Master of the Seal." Brylee watched intently as the pair reached out and clasped each other's forearms–a greeting similar to a handshake but with greater overlap of limbs. She waited to be introduced, but Caelon turned and reached for Brylee's arm without being presented.

"So good to see you again, Genifer," Caelon said. "How is your mother?" Brylee panicked. Was Genifer's mother hale and hearty, or had she recently died of fungusblight? She glanced at Tommus, who smiled warmly, without a hint of warning. Taking his cue, she hoped for the best.

This could be the shortest spy mission in history.

"You're always so kind. She's well," Brylee croaked in Genifer's voice. "But excuse my throat. The healer contained any infection and cured the ache, but could do little for the bark. I look forward to catching up properly over the next few days."

"I completely understand–" Caelon's reply was cut short as Geo Kant pushed her way into the group, grasping the Prime's arm.

"There you are, Caelon," Geo said. Tall and poised, her dark hair fell in soft waves, framing a face that combined beauty with keen intelligence. Her eyes, sharp and perceptive, shone with a quiet strength. She positioned herself just in front of Brylee, forcing her to step back. Brylee was about to get her elbows out but recalled that it didn't serve her to be front and centre, competing for attention.

Brylee recalled that Geo was the Principal Secretary for Mordeland, a position that rotated each year among the three heads of the Trilogy. The Trilogy, the Elect's governing council, consisted of three branches: the Office of the Land, the Office of Military and Enforcement, and the Office of Trade.

This year, Trade held the position of Chair of the Trilogy, making Geo the head of the council. The position gave her frequent access to the Elect and was likely behind the push for the trade conference. Brylee didn't need to be a political savant to see the inherent conflict between Geo's role and Genifer's as the Elect's Wise Councillor of Foreign Affairs. That competitiveness was evidently spilling over here.

The head steward interrupted any further drama with the dinner bell.

"I believe your seat is over there, Genifer," Tommus said, pointing to the long table's corner. With an apologetic smile, he turned and strode off in the other direction.

The dinner went well. After a nervous start, Brylee settled into her corner, made small talk with her table partners, and soaked up as much information as she could. She enjoyed being a fly on the wall. Unable to contribute much due to her feigned illness, she gathered all sorts of personal information from the eight people within earshot, gaining a sense of the issues that would arise in the coming talks. In many ways, it resembled the business she was highly skilled at, yet there were subtleties that she sensed but couldn't fully grasp.

"If you could make your way to the carriages, ladies and gentlemen," announced the chief steward, interrupting Brylee's thoughts.

"It's been a pleasure," Brylee croaked, standing to say her farewells.

"You're not attending the nightcap at the Lord's House?" Darran asked. The lead Thraeven delegate had been aloof all evening, and his sudden switch to a warm, charming tone caught Brylee off guard.

"I'm sure the Wise Councillor won't want to miss the dramatics," Seth Na'var, Nydros's second negotiator, replied. His eyes glistened and his confident tone carried a deliberately theatrical note.

"Dramatics?" Darran asked, retreating into a cooler demeanour, as if the very idea of any such thing was beneath him.

"Of course," Seth smiled and nodded at Brylee as if she knew exactly what he was talking about, then continued. "The shipping issue. We'll have a round of drinks before bed at the Lord's House with the broader delegation staff. Morde's Trilogy leaders will be there, which means Yebba Bane." He stopped talking as if he had explained everything. Brylee recalled that Yebba led the Office of

Military and Enforcement but couldn't see the relevance. She was saved from asking when Darran voiced the same question.

"Well, she won't be at the actual negotiating table, will she? This is her only opportunity to argue with my boss, Jules." When Darran's brow furrowed in confusion, Seth continued. "The key to de-escalation is how we agree to transport our trade. Nydros has an excellent privateer flotilla, and we want that profitable business. Meanwhile, Landar's Guildkin–their cut-throat commerce leaders–want their king to build and pay for transportation, but he's reluctant and thinks it's their responsibility. Geo Kant, on the other hand, wants Mordeland to shift from their 'hire private transport as required' model in favour of building a national merchant navy. Similar to our privateer force, but controlled by her, as part of Mordeland's Office of Trade."

"How does that concern Yebba Bane?" Darran asked, scratching the back of his neck and sighing loudly.

"She wants to build a full-time naval force to protect Mordeland's interests with warships that also carry goods. Geo argues it's too expensive and would discourage trading partners– they won't want warships in their ports. Yebba is desperate to convince my boss to co-fund her proposal, in which Mordeland's military would also protect Nydros's fleet. He's not for it, but Yebba... well, she's not one for accepting opposing views."

Chapter Six

Brylee cornered Tommus on the way to the carriages, surprised to hear she'd be attending a second function that night. He explained that Genifer had already been smuggled over to the Lord's House, and it would complete the deception if Brylee rode over, had a nightcap, and then retired to the room allocated for her and the real Genifer.

"It will give you a chance to inspect the remaining attendees and assess their magical capabilities," he said.

"Your tip said the threat was from one of the Privy Council," Brylee whispered, as he pushed her ahead of him to join the line of delegates collecting their coats before stepping outside.

"Clearly we were wrong, since they were all in the chapel, which you confirmed."

Brylee simmered as the carriage jostled through the dark on the short ride to the Lord's House. She sat next to Geo Kant, whose coolness towards Brylee was palpable. Zan Feelon, Caelon's second negotiator, sat opposite, and Brylee caught him staring at her several times. She resorted to looking out of the window, occasionally touching her throat to remind them she wouldn't be talkative. She needn't have worried. They all seemed content to sit back and listen to the horses' hooves clatter along the cobbled streets.

The Lord's House reception room was bustling with lesser officials, all eager to catch up on what was discussed at dinner and to share their own opinions. The room was brightly lit, prompting most of the women arriving from the palace to visit the powder room to check their faces, while the men made straight for the bar. Brylee joined the latter, intercepting a server with a tray of dark wine, sparing her from queuing.

Brylee took a deep drink, hoping to wash away the annoyance that had plagued her at having to attend. She sighed and turned to survey the room. Yebba Bane stood out immediately—not just because she was as tall as Brylee, more athletic and toned than any other woman present, nor because her bold choice of an off-the-shoulder dress showed off her muscular arms. It wasn't even her aggressive, battle-ready stance that left her surrounded by a wide circle of space which few dared to enter. More than anything, it was the fact that she was a full mage, her solid link to the source shining brightly.

Reflexively, Brylee checked her own shine-shadow—the screen mages and the wise charmers use to dim their aura to that of a normal person. Then she looked around for the Elect. He wasn't present, but she did spot his Master of the Seal lurking guiltily–at least she felt so–in a distant corner. She edged back to stand beside him.

"You didn't mention that one of the Trilogy's leaders is a full mage," Brylee said. Tommus looked down at her glass and she realised she was gripping it so tightly her knuckles were white. She forced herself to relax, mindful of her fiery nature, which had caused her many issues in the past.

"I didn't realise you don't follow court matters closely. It's no secret she has magical power. Her parents are prominent with the Council of Magical Law, but she chose a different path."

"Is she why Jacub isn't in attendance? His known discomfort around our kind?"

"Many will assume so, which is helpful. It provides an excuse to keep him from this environment which is so difficult to protect. Others will convince themselves that he didn't wish to lower himself to mingle with underlings. Quite untrue, but most assume his position makes him aloof and uninterested. It annoys him that people jump to that conclusion, but it serves a purpose today."

Brylee considered that for a moment, then shrugged. Why did she care? She would be out of this mess soon enough. She focused her attention on each person, inspecting their magical capabilities one by one. Aside from herself and Yebba, she identified five other mages in the room. They were representatives from various magical bodies of other nations, as Tommus confirmed.

When Brylee sought out Yebba again, she found her deep in conversation with Jules Gunn, the leader of the Nydros delegation. At first, Brylee expected Yebba to have the ambassador cornered and intimidated, given the intensity she radiated. A crowd, pretending not to be one, circled them at a discreet distance. From where Brylee stood, it was clear that the passionate debate–one Gunn held his own in–had the full attention of those nearby. Seth appeared to be enjoying it, while Zan from Landar looked flushed with anger.

Brylee raised her glass to her lips just as Gunn made his excuses and left Yebba standing, clearly dissatisfied. Brylee felt the same upon discovering her glass was empty. She glanced around, hoping to spot a servant with a tray of refills, but none were close. She took it as a sign that consuming more alcohol wasn't the smartest idea and readied to leave. Looking back at the room, she saw Yebba bearing down on her, eyes filled with determination.

"Refill?" Yebba asked, glancing around but finding no servant either. Her words were slightly slurred. Brylee guessed the wait for the palace diners had been longer than expected, prompting Yebba to drink to quench her ire. Brylee liked her more with every minute, but now wasn't the time, or the body in which to make new friends.

"No, I've got an early start, and the remnants of this tongue-binder," Brylee croaked.

Yebba stepped back and took a long look at Brylee, who fought to steady her aura and suppress the unease in her stomach.

"How did it go with Jules?" Tommus asked, stepping out from the nearby shadows to Brylee's rescue. Yebba looked over at the throng who were presumably discussing her debate in whispers and grunted.

"What's your stance on my navy, Wise Councillor?" Yebba said, ignoring the question. "It's clear what advice Geo gives the Elect, but you are supposed to be the counterpoint, offering alternative views." Brylee didn't want to be drawn in, but she doubted a tough, military type like Yebba would respect her hiding behind a throat infection. She thought back to her own success in building a transportation business for Wispy Weed, which she had expanded to help other farmers.

"If we de-escalate tensions with these talks," Brylee began, "the threat decreases to the point where a costly, large, and dedicated force wouldn't make sense. I imagine navies develop as much heavy brass as an army. In a war, overhead for strategic planning is logical, but to shepherd ships operating on tight margins seems counterintuitive. Then there's the issue of other nations accepting threatening groups into their ports."

Brylee saw Yebba bracing to object and quickly continued.

"However, look at traders who use mercenaries like the Mobi'dern to guard their convoys. Small numbers, relatively low cost, yet fierce and deadly. They're effective, adaptable, and agile. If you propose something nimble, overtly less threatening, with light but professional management, I think you have a strong case. A merchant navy might prioritise profit over combat readiness. If he asked me tonight, that is what I'd tell the Elect."

Yebba stared at Brylee intently, clearly working through her thoughts. Frustration and anger simmered in the woman's vivid green eyes. She broke the tension by cocking her head to the side and huffing loudly.

"And what if tension escalates in the next few days? Then what?" Yebba asked, her tone sharp and unsettling. Brylee hesitated, unsure how to interpret the question or the woman's intensity.

"Well, we're all here to prevent that. Aren't we?" Tommus said. Judging by his granite-like expression, Brylee was sure this was well-trodden ground, debated many times before.

Time to leave, Brylee thought, placing her glass on the bar. She turned and walked away, their voices rising behind her as she flagged down a servant to direct her to her assigned room.

Chapter Seven

Brylee found Genifer in the room assigned to her, where she would remain cloistered in secret for the duration of the talks. It had two beds, a small side room containing night bowls, and cupboards for clothing. Brylee noticed her belongings had been moved from the Linger Longer and unpacked into one of the cupboards. Both women felt the awkwardness of sharing a room while knowing so little about each other, and only one topic was discussed before Brylee blew out the candles.

"How can you be a perfect duplicate of me without a hint of makeup, face putty, or any device I can see?" Genifer asked. Brylee had anticipated the question, and didn't hesitate to throw Gil and Tommus under the cart.

"As we explained earlier, Ghosthand has several of us whom Wickham alters as needed with dark magic," Brylee replied smoothly. "It's not something I'd ask too much about if I were you."

"Did he hurt you?" A pang of guilt rolled over Brylee as Genifer's voice carried genuine concern across the darkness between their beds.

"It's necessary to defend the realm. Wickham is a good man; he ensures I feel as little as possible." She could tell Genifer lay awake for some time after that, but eventually, her breathing slowed, leaving Brylee alone with her own fears.

The chimes of the Lord's House church woke them at sixth bell, and breakfast arrived shortly afterwards. Genifer opened the door while Brylee ducked into the side room. A maid left a full tray on the small table and the two women sat to eat. As they ate, Brylee reviewed the previous evening's talking points while Genifer explained how she expected the upcoming proceedings to unfold.

"You will all sit around a substantial four-sided table, with each nation taking a side. There will be room for four or five attendees each. The Elect will have a seat from which he will open proceedings and attend as he sees fit. He's deeply invested in these affairs, so he'll likely be present and attentive. While he often appears bored and as if his mind wanders, don't be fooled–he misses little.

"Geo Kant will sit to his left, alongside an aide or two. She'll lead most of the speaking for Mordeland. The seat to Jacub's right is reserved for key leaders, depending on the topic at hand. Vault Keeper Stonebridge will often sit in, as trade and coffers are so intimately linked, but others will rotate depending on the session's focus.

"You will sit one row back, at the Elect's right shoulder. He may turn and ask for advice, typically an alternate opinion on Geo's position. This will be the hardest part for you; you don't have the experience to contribute effectively."

"What should I say, then?" Brylee asked.

Genifer paused, her lips pursed, and brows furrowed.

"If it seems appropriate, ask for time to consider, and come to me. Be mindful of the body language around the table, and not just of those speaking. There are very few topics that involve only two parties. Trade awarded to one nation means trade lost by two others. Support Geo's position if you are forced into an immediate answer. I don't see eye-to-eye with her on all matters, but she knows her business and puts the nation first."

They spent the next bell and a half thoroughly reviewing the day's agenda until a firm knock interrupted them. Brylee opened the door while Genifer hid out of sight. It was Tommus's aide, delivering instructions for Brylee to attend a brief meeting with Wickham and the Master of the Seal. Gathering her notes, since she would head directly to the first session afterward, she followed him down the corridor.

"We've completed an initial investigation of the Faith Keeper's death," Tommus said, as they crowded into the small room allotted to him. "Your theories have been confirmed, although I doubt we would have arrived at the same conclusion had you not suggested we examine those details. We spoke to everyone who had business in that part of the palace, but no one recalls seeing anything unusual."

"Nothing unusual, but there were people there who would typically be present?" Brylee asked.

"Yes, other guards, palace staff, and so on. But no one noticed anyone loitering near the chapel, ready to tear down the arch as the ceremony ended."

"Someone was there, though," Brylee said. "Either someone who belonged there or someone who simply went unnoticed. Perhaps both."

"How would someone go unnoticed?" Tommus asked. "It's a well-lit area with few places to hide."

"Are you implying the assassin is a mage who can make themselves invisible?" asked Wickham, his question drawing a worried glance from Tommus.

"Invisibility isn't impossible," Brylee replied. "It can be achieved by bending light, like a mirror. But I've never seen anyone capable of maintaining it while moving. Standing still in a corner is one thing; moving around the palace unseen would be impossible."

"Then why ask?"

"It's a very rare skill, but it is possible to influence people's minds. Make them forget what they saw or steer their attention away without them realising they're being manipulated."

"How rare? Could *you* do it?" Tommus asked.

Brylee only knew of her husband, Levi, but she would never reveal his unique abilities to someone like Tommus. She could tell by Wickham's face he had deduced to whom she referred.

"I couldn't, no. But I believe it can be done," Brylee said.

"They call me Ghosthand, but invisibility—" Tommus rubbed his temples and screwed his eyes shut. "That would make it impossible to catch our man."

"Probably," Brylee said. "But not definitely. It's very rare and effective, but seldom flawless. The mind is complex; memories are often interlinked. As I understand it, one might erase the sight of a meal from a man's mind, but he might recall smelling the gravy. It's a long shot, but ask people for any sense of oddness from that night. Did they arrive somewhere and forget why they were there? Did they have moments of déjà vu? Recall greeting someone but not seeing them? Anything strange."

Tommus looked sceptical but agreed to follow up. Brylee had a question of her own.

"I feel vulnerable masquerading as Genifer so close to the Elect. I appreciate you will be there most of the time, but what if I am exposed while you're away? What if I'm forced to act to protect the Elect, and people think I'm part of an attack? I'm wondering if we should tell the Elect or at least Sim Glay about my role?"

"Absolutely not," Tommus replied. "Jacub would never permit it. And Sim's so damn honourable he'd feel compelled to tell the Elect. It just won't work."

"Then I'm not sure I want to go ahead with this. It's been worrying me all night." The Master of the Seal stepped towards her, drawing himself up to his full height. His attempt at intimidation faltered against Brylee's broad shoulders and unyielding stance.

"What if Ghosthand wrote you a note of employment? With his seal? You could hide it on your person and present it in an emergency," Wickham said quickly, attempting to defuse the confrontation before it began. Brylee considered the suggestion. It seemed a fair compromise. She nodded.

Five minutes later, with the note folded close to her chest, she followed Tommus into the Lord's House meeting chambers and took her seat behind the Elect's chair, waiting for his grand entrance.

Chapter Eight

By lunchtime, Brylee's fears of being exposed when asked for her opinion had subsided–the Elect hadn't turned in his chair since wishing her good morning. Yet, she was far from bored. Her experience running several businesses of her own and serving on Haxley's town council gave her enough insight to grasp the chess game playing out at the table.

The Thraevens were aggressive, often outright hostile. They claimed an alliance with Backalar–who had pulled out of the conference–but some deft questioning by Jules Gunn of Nydros neatly exposed their bluff. Jules hadn't pressed to the point of humiliating the Thraevens but his intervention had left them visibly weakened.

Caelon of Landar offered lower prices, on the condition that her proposed merchant armada carried not only their own goods but also those of other nations at a premium. Mordeland pushed back, citing concerns that the delivery sequence would favour others. Privately, however, Genifer had shared that Mordeland intended to make the same play for shipping rights later in the talks.

In a rare intervention, Jacub voiced his support for Yebba's naval plan. Brylee didn't think him much of a diplomat. His clumsily phrased points raised the room's temperature. *He wasn't helping his cause of de-escalating trade issues.*

The Nydros delegates mostly remained quiet, stepping in quickly to calm the mood when needed. They offered fair terms and poked holes in the more egregious claims made by Landar and the aggressive Thraevens. Their unique products such as complex timepieces, rare alloys, and exotic chemicals made them indispensable. They favoured a strategy of being an honest broker, with the subtle threat of withholding their products to press for civility in all dealings.

Brylee began to sense Mordeland and Nydros were working in tandem. Nydros was the anvil-steady and unmovable. Mordeland was the hammer, wielding more goods and buying power. Subtly, between them, they were beating down and removing the restrictive and punitive deals that existed today, replacing them with less volatile, fairer terms.

They worked through lunch and adjourned promptly at fifteenth bell. Brylee sensed that the negotiations aligned with the Elect's overall plan, but that today was merely the opening round of skirmishes. She looked forward to debriefing with Genifer to verify her observations and better prepare her for the following day's strategy.

"Come to my chambers," Jacub Morde said, turning in his chair for the first time. "You too," he said to Geo. Though he didn't specifically include Sim Glay, the loyal bodyguard followed closely, his hand resting on his sword. Brylee was impressed the man had stood silently for the entire proceedings, never once appearing bored.

The Master of the Seal wasn't included, and his face bore a concerned frown as his eyes met Brylee's while she walked out. She reminded herself to mimic Genifer's graceful movements rather than falling into her own assertive gait.

Bernart appeared to anticipate their arrival, opening the door to the large suite the Elect occupied in the Lord's House just as they approached. He handed the Elect a steaming cup of tea as he entered. Brylee suppressed a childish smirk at Bernart's title, King's Stool, though she admitted the odd designation suited the dapper man. His dignified demeanour made him immune to mocking, elevating him above such pettiness, leaving others feeling guilty and inferior.

As Brylee filed in, she felt Bernart's eyes on her. His face remained humble and deferential, but his quick glance took her in completely. Her throat tightened. It was the unmistakable look of a mage scanning someone with their magical sight–his eyes a fraction unfocused, as if looking beyond her. He casually picked away a fleck of thread on his impeccable uniform.

He has a subtle cunning and probably more influence than most recognise, Brylee intuited.

Sim Glay surprised Brylee by noticeably relaxing once he had spoken to the two guards stationed in the corridor. Closing the door behind them, he loosened his belt and slipped his weapons off, placing them next to a seat near the doorway. Stretching his shoulders several times, he lowered himself into a chair.

Geo took a step towards Bernart, her hand rising as if to touch his arm. It would have been a subtle, intimate gesture, Brylee imagined, had it landed. Instead, she saw a flicker of recognition of what was about to happen in the man's eyes, before she became aware of a vague sensation she hadn't felt in years. Geo's arm dropped, and she turned away.

He smudged her! In her early years working for Wickham she had trained as a spy. Her mentor, Winter, had taught her the art of projecting certain vibes to influence those around her. Perhaps to attract them without their knowledge, or to deflect, as Bernart had just demonstrated. Most people had this ability at some unconscious level, but Winter had taught her how to make it a craft. While magic could certainly enhance the ability, it was by no means essential.

Did Bernart not want her that close under these circumstances? Or in any? Are they secret lovers or was he rebuffing unwanted advances?

Brylee reminded herself that Bernart was inside the chapel during the assassination attempt. It was hard to believe a charmer's enhanced smudging ability could cause such mayhem. Yet in some circumstances, such covert influence could subtly alter the course of major decisions.

"Let's debrief," the Elect said, pulling Brylee from her musings. Bernart moved to the table and lifted metal covers from the dishes. She noted most of the dishes were arranged at the right-hand end of the table, but a single tray sat at the left, a yellow flower in a small vase in its corner. Brylee recalled Ghosthand explaining the flower signalled that the Elect's taster had sampled everything on the tray for poison and deemed them safe.

Once the Elect was seated, they all chose a chair, and Geo began a concise summary of events while the food was distributed and the wine poured. No one touched their plates, waiting for the Elect to start. Bernart was clearly a man of great precision. He squared up each item on everyone's tray and ensured everything was presented just so. It seemed customary for him to serve the Elect's guests before delivering Jacub's tray.

Brylee was surprised to find she was able to contribute several small observations to complement the Principal Secretary's summary. The woman didn't seem to mind, nodding to each, and even praising her on one suggestion. It occurred to Brylee that none of her comments mattered in the big picture. Worse, she risked exposing herself by saying something that might upset some hornet's nest. She admonished herself, resolving to remain quiet unless asked a question.

As she settled back, a fleeting flicker tugged at her peripheral vision. A shadow, perhaps, or the briefest ripple of air where nothing should be. She turned towards it, but the area was empty. She felt the hairs on the back of her neck rise and glanced at Sim Glay, who was staring at his plate, clearly ravenous.

Brylee peered at the spot where she thought she had seen something. It was near Geo, but Bernart had stepped between them, the Elect's tray in hand. She wasn't sure. She trusted her instincts. Her gut told her it was a flicker her magical sight had caught, not her eyes. She switched and saw magical energy swirling in front of her in tiny amounts. As she followed it back to its source, two things happened simultaneously: Bernart hurled the tray to the floor with a crash, and Brylee's magical sense passed through the wall behind Geo and saw one of the biggest links to the source she had ever encountered. Whoever lurked outside the chamber was a mage of enormous power.

As the room erupted, Brylee threw up a wall of hard air between the Elect and the unseen intruder.

"This food is poisoned," Bernart gasped.

A moment later, Brylee felt an overwhelming pressure bear down on the shield she had erected. She had anchored it to both the wall and the floor, and as the intruder pressed, Brylee threw all of her power into preventing it from shattering.

One wave struck. Then another. The third crashed against it with brutal force and her vision greyed at the edges as she gripped the arms of her chair.

Suddenly the pressure ceased, leaving Brylee panting and drenched with sweat. With everyone focused on Bernart no one seemed to notice her struggle.

Grabbing her napkin, she dabbed at her face. There was a tall mirror the Elect used to dress at her side, and she quickly checked if her disguise had held together under the onslaught. It hadn't entirely. Her hair had faded to towards its natural light brown, and she quickly darkened it again.

Through her magical sight, Brylee followed the massive link as it moved along the corridor behind the wall. She considered following, but stopped herself. Leaving the room might throw suspicion on her for poisoning the Elect's meal. She watched as the link merged into the crowd in an adjacent room, winking out and vanishing completely.

Chapter Nine

"The gravy on your potatoes, I'd say, sire," Bernart said, carefully scooping the fallen food back onto the tray. He had removed his white gloves and replaced them with an older pair to preserve the set he used daily.

"The colour is off, and I believe I smell ghost-lily and frostmoss spores." Everyone set their meals aside, fearful of poisoning.

"Gravy comes in many shades, depending on the chef's whim," Geo argued. "Are you sure it's poisoned? Mine smells like regular gravy." Bernart stood with his back ramrod straight and looked down his nose at her.

"Principal Secretary, I know how the Elect likes his meals. His personal chef prepared this in the kitchens below, using ingredients from the palace garden. The balance of roasted marrow bones and charred duck juices should result in a shade like well-worn leather, neither too dark nor too pale. And that slight shimmer on the surface? That tells you it's been kissed by fire, but never scorched. If it were any lighter, you'd know it lacked the depth, and any darker, you'd taste the bitterness. Perfect, except for these thin white rivulets, like poorly processed mushroom stalks, which should not be there."

Brylee studied her own plate, noting that the gravy and meat were quite different, presumably served by the Lord's House chefs. Her magical sight couldn't pinpoint the exact makeup of the white streaks Bernart had described, but she had seen naether shift near the Elect's tray and didn't doubt his precise analysis.

"I carried this tray from the kitchen myself after the taster approved it. No one has been close to it, I am certain. We should check whether your taster still breathes, sir," Bernart said.

Sim Glay sent one guard to the kitchen and the other to fetch the Master of the Seal. The first returned with the Elect's personal chef and taster just as Tommus stepped into the room. He shot a glance at Brylee before rushing to the Elect's side.

The next half-bell was full of questions no one could answer. When replacement food arrived, there was a failed attempt to resume the original discussion. Eventually, an unsettled Jacub Morde dismissed them, asking them to return a bell before the talks resumed in the morning. Brylee positioned herself to leave after Geo and saw the woman's eyes linger on Bernart's back with a wistful expression as he tidied things away.

Tommus escorted Brylee back to his small room, where Wickham was waiting. The mage, familiar with the intricacies of the links that convey naether, thanks to his interactions with Brylee and Levi, had a keen understanding of their power. Most mages had only a fraction of such knowledge.

Not wanting to share too much with Ghosthand, Brylee limited her account to stating that she had sensed magic in the room and detected a powerful mage behind the wall.

"And you say the mage simply disappeared?" Tommus asked. "Like magic? I feel foolish asking, but is that unusual?"

"Very," Brylee replied. "If I'm focused, I can see a living aura from dozens of strides away, even through most obstructions. I can't always tell who they belong to unless there is something unique about them, such as this man's immense power. Right now, if I spread my senses, I can detect perhaps a hundred lifeforces in this part of the Lord's House. Imagine each one like a candle in the dark. But unlike a candle, a light that large cannot simply be snuffed out."

"What do you mean?" Tommus asked.

"When someone dies, their light fades over several seconds; it's more like an ember cooling than putting one's thumb on a wick."

"And is it unusual to be able to poison food? Through a wall?" Tommus asked.

Wickham spoke before Brylee could. "I could probably do it with some practice. For a mage adept at transforming things, changing the substance wouldn't be the issue. The real challenge is being able to see precisely enough through a wall to locate the gravy, especially on a moving plate. Food doesn't glow like a candle because it isn't alive."

Noticing Tommus's puzzled look, he continued. "Mages aren't so different from non-mages. Some people are good at fighting but hopeless cooks. Others might be great with horses, but poor swimmers. Similarly, some mages can make air hard or manipulate heat and cold, but struggle to change other properties."

A tap at the door interrupted them. Tommus stepped out, and Brylee heard low voices. She took the moment to expand on what she had observed to Wickham.

"Gil, this mage's link was huge. I can't recall seeing one like it. If it's within a hundred strides now, I should still be able to see it clearly."

"I'm surprised you managed to fend it off. No offence," Wickham said, shuffling awkwardly as he realised the unintended insult.

"Had the man possessed any real skill, it would have been a different outcome," Brylee said. "Raw power but coarsely controlled. A heavy weight of air, where a needle, a spear, or heat would have been far more effective."

They broke off their conversation as Ghosthand stepped back into the room and shut the door.

"I've placed many eyes around the Lord's House, as you can imagine," Tommus said. "I just received a report of suspicious activity."

He went to his wardrobe and opened the door, retrieving several rolled-up maps and fumbling through them until he found the one he wanted. He spread it out on the table, weighing down the corners with water cups. It was a diagram of the part of the building containing the Elect's rooms.

"Here is Jacub's suite," he said, tracing a finger across the map as Brylee and Wickham looked over his shoulder. "And this is the adjacent corridor from where the attacker struck, leading from the stairs down to the archives and on to the transient servants' quarters. The passageway would be quiet, as the archivist's activities are suspended during the talks. You said the assassin fled to your right? That would take them through the servants' quarters."

"What are transient servants?" Brylee asked.

"The staff who serve Lord Welsham are housed permanently on the other side of the property, near his lordship. The wing we occupy houses delegations who stay temporarily while concluding their business, and they are allotted suites, as we have been. Their servants need somewhere to sleep near their employers. They are considered transient because they only stay for a short while."

"The guests this week are from so many places they would all be strangers to each other," Wickham said. "Someone could move through unnoticed if dressed appropriately."

"Quite so," replied Tommus. "But I have a report of one person moving through there at the time of the attack who seemed out of place. Our Keeper of the Vault, Wenowar Stonebridge. She claimed she was lost when asked if she needed help. A footman directed her back to her room, yet my man saw her heading towards the area where the foreign delegates are billeted instead."

"Did they see which room she went into?" Wickham asked.

"Unfortunately, not. My instruction was to observe, not follow."

"Stonebridge doesn't possess any magic," Brylee reminded them.

"But was it truly Wenowar?" Tommus asked. "An assassin doesn't need as complete a disguise as you've achieved to blend among strangers."

Brylee thought for a few moments, and a plan occurred to her.

"Can you get me a servant's uniform in my size?" she asked. "I'll spend some time near the guests' quarters and see if I can come up with anything."

"Won't you be recogni–" Tommus began, but the words died in his mouth as Brylee began to alter her appearance. In a previous adventure, she had spent years switching between several characters and now selected one that suited her needs. Before his eyes, her features broadened, her skin darkened, and her hair became black and frizzy.

"Dear Ag," Tommus cried, taking a long step back and raising a hand to his face.

"It's quite unsettling," Wickham agreed, having seen Brylee's talent before. "You don't get used to it."

Half a bell later, Brylee, now disguised as "Scarlet" from the Archipelago Islands, was dusting the ledges along the guest wing passageways. There was no sign of Wenowar.

When her presence in that area started to draw attention, she sought a hiding place. At the end of the main corridor was a large skylight over a small vestibule, from which smaller hallways branched off to clusters of rooms assigned to each delegation. The skylight had decorative stonework behind which she could hide. Brylee waited until the corridor was empty, then created a set of hard air stairs, climbing up and dismissing them once she was concealed. She settled in to watch.

From her perch, Brylee could see most of the doors to the Thraeven and Nydros suites, but not those leading to the Landar quarters. As the evening turned to night, the traffic below her slowed, and the nightman came through, blowing out several candles and replacing others with long-burning tallow versions that had a bluer tinge. Brylee shifted several times to ease cramps and to keep herself from dozing off.

A raised voice pulled her attention back to the corridor as the door to Seth's rooms was jerked open. A tall, thickset man in a hooded cloak stepped out, then turned back to the doorway. He raised his hands, as if to say something, but Nydros's second negotiator's voice cut him off.

"No, we won't. Even on those terms." Seth pushed the door closed to prevent further argument, and Brylee heard the lock snap shut like a final punctuation mark.

The figure turned and adjusted his hood, giving Brylee a glimpse of the wearer's face in the dim light. She was surprised to see it wasn't a man's face, as she'd expected. Yebba Bane's symmetrical features and sharp jawline were unmistakable, but the expression was ambiguous. Brylee couldn't decide if it was conniving or relieved as the leader of Mordeland's military strode down the corridor.

Brylee ducked back behind the stonework as Yebba glanced her way. She heard the woman's steps falter, then continue until they faded with distance.

Brylee's mind worked through the puzzle for some time, but eventually, her eyes became unbearably heavy. She was considering calling it a night when another door below her cracked open, and a man's face peeked out. Seeing the hallway was clear, he opened the door fully, revealing the Keeper of the Vault stepping into full view. Brylee eased herself higher. Darran Midros closed the door silently, leaving the woman alone in the dim light.

Wenowar adjusted her clothing, patted her hair to ensure everything was in place, then walked confidently towards the main meeting areas. Once she was out of sight, Brylee dropped down silently and followed. She trailed the woman through the rooms assigned to the Mordeland delegation, watching as Wenowar disappeared into a suite bearing her title. Brylee continued past and soon knocked on the door marked Master of the Seal.

Brylee accepted some crackers and cheese along with a glass of wine. Her mouth felt woolly from the dust in the skylight. She explained her observations to Tommus and Wickham.

"Wenowar doesn't have a trace of magic in her," she said. "It's possible there is a different issue at play, but she is not our assassin. I'm certain."

"What was she doing there?" Wickham asked.

"She emerged from Midros's room, glowing and smoothing her dress. I recall Genifer mentioning our Keeper of the Vault spent a lot of time in Thraeven when she was younger. I suspect she was renewing old acquaintances. She could have been spilling state secrets, I suppose, but I'd wager she is in good humour come morning."

Tommus paced as he thought things through, eventually agreeing Wenowar was an unlikely assassin.

"What about Yebba?" Brylee asked. "She's magical and clearly acting suspiciously. That was no romantic rendezvous I witnessed."

"Clearly not," Tommus replied. "But she is scheduled to leave for the south on a border inspection tour at first light. She's no threat if she isn't here."

His response didn't sit well with Brylee, partly because of his dismissive tone. She had expected him to be more curious.

"But Bernart was right about the poison," Tommus continued. "Some sort of strangler derivative that my poison master couldn't identify. The King's Stool certainly has a sharp nose."

"I doubt it's his nose," Brylee replied. When the two men looked at her for an explanation, she said, "It's because he's a charmer. He probably thinks he's smelling something, but I suspect his mind is enhancing his senses in ways he doesn't even realise."

She paused, then asked, "Is there anything between Bernart and the Principal Secretary?" She explained the odd interaction she'd observed at the start of the last meeting in Jacub's suite.

"Nothing I know of," Tommus replied, "but it's another thing to add to my ever-growing list of oddities to investigate."

They spoke for a short while but were no closer to identifying the assassin. One thing was certain: the Elect was lucky to be alive. And after several failed attempts, the assassin was likely to grow bolder.

Chapter Ten

Magram confirmed the corridor was empty before magically extinguishing all but one of the candles. The boards underfoot creaked softly, and the lock on Genifer's room clicked as the tumblers yielded to magical persuasion.

Two women lay asleep, one lightly and the other soundly. Magram adjusted a magical knot to allow slightly more energy to flow from the source than the typical restricted trickle. Using the surplus, Magram reached out to finesse the sleepers' minds. By gently agitating the small area above their brainstems, the mage released chemicals to deepen their sleep into a dream state. Warming a small spot in the frontal area of their brains ensured those dreams were vivid and distracting. They would not wake until released.

The resemblance between the two women was astonishing, even with prior warning. Magram could easily kill them both, but refrained, partly because it was unclear which was Genifer and which was the imposter, and partly because the time was not right. An order had been given; the imposter would live to take the blame when the Elect fell.

But who is this pretender that thwarted my mission?

Magram sat carefully on the edge of the first bed and touched the woman's cheek. An oddity among mages, Magram could not see a person's link at all, and barely their aura, unless in physical contact.

Nothing. Magram fully relaxed the knot that stemmed the flow of magic at the source, allowing the link to flood and expand. The rush of power was intoxicating after surviving on the minimum for hours, like gulping down lungsful of fresh air after being trapped in a confined, smoky space. Gripping the woman's cheek tighter revealed no sense of power in her, so Magram relaxed and caressed the pinched flesh with a gentle touch. *I'm sorry.*

Magram stood, moved to the far side of the second bed, perched on its edge, and touched the other woman's cheek—using the left hand, as a defect in the right shoulder made it easier to reach out. On contact with the second Genifer, the difference was unmistakable; this woman swam with power. Magram still could not see the link with any clarity, but there was no doubt. This was the fake, the Trickster, the enemy. The hand that touched the woman's cheek dropped to her throat, encircling it firmly.

It wouldn't do to bruise you, Trickster. Not yet. But soon, I will wring the life from you. Once that monster Jacub is ash and bone.

A hastily penned note, found hidden in the woman's clothing on the chair by the bed, revealed the imposter and her role in matters.

One of Ghosthand's spectres. I doubt she can match my full power. Who can? But she is evidently clever. Intellectual. I have to rely on cunning, not intelligence. Perhaps it would be safer if I kill her now.

It took half a bell before Magram decided that the Trickster would breathe for a few more hours.

Magram drifted from the room, releasing the sleepers and magically sparked the candles back to life, jerked the knot tight, winnowing the surplus naether down to the smallest trickle–just enough to loosen it again when needed.

Magram drifted from the room and released the sleepers. With a melodramatic hand motion, the candles sparked back to life. Then came the final step: jerking the knot tight and winnowing the surplus naether down to the smallest trickle-just enough to loosen it again when needed.

Magram hurried back to the foreign delegates' suites to report and to plead for permission to kill the Trickster along with the Elect before the day was out.

I shouldn't have to beg. But once this is over, I'll be free.

Chapter Eleven

Brylee woke with a start, seizing upon an idea that had come to her in a dream. She dressed quickly and slipped from the room, leaving Genifer to her slumber. The corridors in her wing of the Lord's House were empty, and as she passed by the entrance to the Elect's suites, she noted the alert guards, but something felt off. She paused as realisation struck.

She continued through the ornate passageways and soon spotted the aides seated outside the Master of the Seal's suite, always ready to do his bidding. She knocked softly, unsurprised when he opened it at once.

"We are going about this all wrong," she said, pushing into the room. The Master of the Seal, not yet dressed for the day, tightened the cord of his nightrobe. He raised an eyebrow as Brylee helped herself to a slice of his toasted bread and spread it with honey.

"Do explain to me how my strategy is incorrect," he said, making no effort to hide his sarcasm.

"I'm taking a great risk, but so is the realm. If our aim is to prevent war by de-escalating tensions, the Elect needs his most trusted advisors at his side. The real Wise Councillor needs to be in the room with him."

"Then how do we keep him alive? You've already saved him once."

"That's the point. I'm only with him during the meetings. What if the assassin strikes while he is asleep or at dinner?"

"I've taken precautions," Tommus replied.

"Posting guards outside the suite at night didn't fool me. And it won't fool our assassin into thinking the Elect is there. Did you move him to the palace, or just switch him to another room of the Lord's House?" A rare look of surprise rippled across Ghosthand's face before it vanished, replaced by a wry smile.

"The Palace. How did you know?"

"I wasn't sure, but you're too smart to leave him exposed to a mage who can strike through walls and then disappear. And I expected to see Sim Glay guarding the Elect's door as I walked past just now. Dawn approaches, the prime time for attack–and he would know that. My magical sight can see only one person inside the suite, so Sim's not in there protecting his charge."

"Even Glay has to sleep."

"Yes, but not at dawn, and not when the Elect is so vulnerable. It just doesn't make sense."

"Very clever. Do you believe the Elect is at risk at the palace? Our intelligence says the threat comes from one of the delegations, and they are all accounted for here."

"They waltzed through the palace, attacked the Elect at the chapel, and left without being seen. Again, you are too smart to not know that, so he must be somewhere other than his palace chambers." Tommus began to pace slowly, running his hand through his thinning grey hair.

"Do you have a better idea?"

"Only one. I agree you need to play this shell game with the Elect's whereabouts—but put me at his side constantly, not just here."

"But the Elect doesn't know you. He'll never agree to your presence—" A sharp intake of breath cut Ghosthand off mid-sentence, and he froze in his tracks. Brylee slowly morphed from her Genifer disguise into a replica of Sim Glay, a shocking sight on its own, made even more unsettling in a woman's clothing.

"And Glay rarely speaks. Who better for me to impersonate?" Brylee said. "All I have to do is follow the Elect around and glare at anyone who gets too close. He's never more than a few steps from the man you want me to protect."

Tommus sat on the end of his bed, crossed his arms, and stroked his chin. Brylee helped herself to the rest of his toasted bread and let him think.

"I admit it's quite brilliant, but Sim would never agree to it."

"Why not? He must realise he can't defend the Elect against such a talented mage. Surely, he isn't so full of pride that he'd refuse to accept a better option."

"No, pride wouldn't stop him, but his loyalty would. He wouldn't desert his post without Jacub's permission. He would insist we tell the Elect, and the Elect won't tolerate a mage hovering around him all day. He would rather cancel the talks or claim illness and hand them over to the Principal Secretary."

"Perhaps that would be for the best," Brylee said. "But if we were going to tell the Elect, we can do even better." Brylee smiled as her face slowly changed to that of Jacub Morde's.

"Dear Ag, no!" Tommus said, shaking his head. "The man is already paranoid that one day a mage will take his throne. He'd never allow it."

A soft knock interrupted them. Tommus waited as Brylee reverted to Genifer's form, then cracked open the door before pulling it wider to admit Wickham.

The Master of the Seal wasted no time explaining Brylee's idea.

"She's not wrong," Wickham said. "The Elect would be safer with her at his side than Sim in these circumstances. What if we fooled the Elect?"

"What do you mean?" Tommus asked.

"Go to Jacub and tell him we have proof the gravy was transformed magically, and share the evidence of the other magical attempts on his life. Say I have a mage who looks very similar to Glay, close enough he could be his brother, but with some makeup and dyed hair, could fool almost anyone. He'd still despise having a mage nearby, but might allow it to ease international tensions. Especially if I vouched for the mage. And if he doesn't agree, Brylee continues to play Genifer."

A bell later, after much debate and another full breakfast delivered from the kitchen, Tommus left to seek the Elect's permission to substitute 'his spy' for Sim Glay. By now, Jacub had likely returned to his suite at the Lord's House, enjoying his morning meal served by Bernart.

Brylee once again transformed herself into the spitting image of the Elect's Master at Arms. She then refined the disguise, narrowing her cheeks, brightening the area around her eyes, and lengthening and lightening her hair. Holding up a set of men's clothing Tommus had retrieved from his wardrobe, she prepared to change, prompting Wickham to turn his back. They both agreed that, despite her male disguise, it would be inappropriate for him to watch.

Tommus was gone so long they were beginning to lose hope. Then the door finally opened, and a red-faced Master of the Seal waved for Brylee to follow. They left Wickham pacing nervously around Ghosthand's room.

"It didn't go well," Tommus admitted as they marched briskly through the passageways. "We ended up yelling at each other. I offered my resignation, claiming his "discriminatory attitudes" were preventing me from doing my job of keeping him alive and protecting the realm. He accepted, arguing that I'd called him prejudiced. I'm still not sure if I'm in his employ, or not."

"So what changed his mind?"

"I'm not sure it has changed. Surprisingly, Sim Glay supported me. He's fearless, of course, but he admitted he wasn't well-equipped to protect Jacub under these circumstances. The Elect remained firmly against the idea until Bernart, of all people, asked if Wickham had vouched for you."

"And Wickham has at least some of the Elect's trust. I'll have to get the story behind that one day."

"Good luck with that. Bernart then suggested the Elect see you with his own eyes before making the final decision. But there is a condition, I'm afraid."

"One I won't like?"

"Glay is to keep his sword at your throat in case you try anything."

"I'm not worried about that," Brylee said, with a wry grin. "I'm not about to make any sudden moves, and it may play to our advantage.

Sim Glay met them at the door to the Elect's suite, and Brylee gave him credit for barely reacting to the sight of someone who looked so much like himself.

"We must be related," Glay said, as he patted Brylee down for hidden weapons. Satisfied, he led her inside. With an apologetic nod, he unsheathed his dagger and placed its tip against the large Adam's apple Brylee had recently created.

Tommus followed them in but kept his distance, settling near the door to observe.

Jacub Morde looked up from his breakfast, setting aside an official-looking document he had been combing through.

"Ag, you two do look alike. Is there a family connection?"

"No, sir," Brylee replied in a close approximation of Glay's deep baritone.

"And you're one of Ghosthand's foxes, are you?"

"No, sir. One of Gil Wickham's, actually." Brylee hoped to build trust on that slim branch of honesty.

"And you'd be prepared to put yourself between me and an assassin with magical abilities? Do you think you could fight another mage?"

"You made a law against mages learning to fight, sir. But I suspect I could hold my own, if it came to it." Brylee winced internally, knowing that reminding the Elect of his paranoid laws was a mistake. He stood, pushing his chair back, scrubbing at his forearms as if he had a rash.

"Exactly," he said. His lip curled, and he swallowed hard, his mouth dry. "No. It's not that I don't appreciate the gesture. I'm sure you are brave and serve Wickham well, but I'll not have a mage around me all day." He brushed his palms against his tunic and went to sit down.

"Of course, sir. You don't have to accept me, but Wickham would be angry at me if I failed to point out that there is a good chance you will have a mage near you all day."

"Or I could see you thrown in the dungeons," Jacub said, his voice raised.

"Oh, I don't mean me, sir. I meant the enemy mage. Seems to come and go as he pleases." Brylee looked at Glay and offered an apologetic shrug. "And if you'll allow me to make one last point about your safety before I go, sir?" The Elect's face flushed and he pressed his lips together. He glared but waved her to proceed.

Brylee whispered a prayer, filled with deep anxiety about the consequences of what she was about to do.

"It's my belief that everyone in this room has spurned mages to such an extent that none of you have any idea how truly dangerous we are." As she spoke, she sealed the door, rendering it impervious to sound and entry. She wrapped everyone but herself in a column of air, trapping them in place. Then, as if taking a casual stroll, she stepped clear of Glay's dagger and walked slowly towards the Elect's desk. His eyes bulged as he attempted to get away from her.

"You are wrong to mistrust all mages. We are no different from non-magical people. Some of us are loyal and of high moral character, while others are less trustworthy, but no more so than ordinary people. Bernart may be skilled in poisons, but can he or Sim protect you from an ordinary man concealing a poison dart tube in his sleeve? Or a Mobi'dern warrior?"

The Elect had turned such a dark shade of red Brylee double-checked she hadn't inadvertently cut off his air supply. She switched to her magical sight and, using her knowledge of healing, assessed the likelihood of him suffering heart failure. He wasn't far from it. In fact, she noticed he had so much fatty tissue clogging his veins, he didn't have a bright future without intervention. This revelation encouraged her to proceed.

Tommus, Glay, and Bernart struggled without success against the bonds she had created. Brylee ignored them as she selected a sheet of royal note paper and a quill, taking her time to write a lengthy note. When she had finished, she blotted the ink and blew on it before folding the paper in half.

"Gentlemen, please relax. I'm not here to hurt anyone. I'm just trying to show you how ill-equipped you are to take on someone magical, determined, and with knowledge of your environment. I will release you, unharmed, in one moment." Her words didn't help much, and all three continued to struggle against her restraints.

Brylee picked up a small silver tray from the desk and put the note on it, then stepped over to where Bernart stood. She placed the tray on a small table beside him and retreated to the farthest corner of the room from the Elect. She shoved her hands deep into her pockets, and leaned back against the wall.

"Bernart," she said, "I'll release you so you can place the note in front of the Elect. I think he might burst a blood vessel if I go near him."

She allowed the air around the man to soften gradually, ensuring he didn't fall after his earlier struggle to break free. When he was steady, he took a step towards Brylee, but she halted him with a simple wave of her hand.

"The note, Bernart," she said. Bernart glared at her and the tray, and with great effort, brought himself under control. He rolled his shoulders, as if expelling the remaining anger from his body, then straightened his clothing. Once he had regained a measure of composure, he picked up the tray and walked across the room to place it in front of the Elect.

"Good. Thank you," Brylee said. "Now, sir. I'll free you next, so you can read my note. After that, I'll release everyone else." She waited a few moments to let the Elect process her words before slowly relaxing her grip on him. Once he felt he was free, he grabbed the note, bolted from his chair to the corner of the room, and hunched over, breathing rapidly.

Brylee removed her hands from her pockets and raised them, palms forward, empty.

Jacub Morde caught his breath, glowered at Brylee, and then at her note. He unfolded it and read it twice, then continued to stare at it. Brylee released Glay and Tommus but kept the room sealed to prevent any sudden outbursts complicating matters.

Glay surprised Brylee with how fast he could move in his light armour. He crossed the room to where she stood so quickly that she barely had time to react and erect a barrier around herself. A breath before Glay got to her, the Elect called out.

"Stop!" Glay barely registered the Elect's words, but when they penetrated his anger, he slammed his foot down to halt his momentum. He kept his dagger pointed towards Brylee as he pivoted slightly to look at Jacub Morde, who had one hand raised towards him and continued, "Stand down, Sim. Give me a moment, would you?"

"I didn't bring you in here to attack the Elect," shouted Tommus, stepping forward. Released from his hard air prison, he shook with shock and anger. Brylee knew she had burned several bridges with the man.

"You were fired anyway," Brylee said, trying to defuse his fury. Seeing his anger deepen, she added, "I'm sorry, Tommus. I'm just trying to save our leader from himself."

"Shut up. All of you," Jacub said. He reread the note before folding it and tucking it into his pocket. He straightened his jacket and looked at Bernart. "How long until my first appointment?" Jacub asked.

"Your Principal Secretary should be here shortly, sir," Bernart replied. The Elect turned to Brylee.

"Your name?"

"Nalik," she replied, startled that her late brother's name had sprung to her lips. She only hoped Tommus hadn't given the Elect a fake name that Jacub had forgotten in the drama.

"Nalik, can you be ready to take Sim's place in a bell's time? Do you even know how to hold a sword?" Jacub asked.

"If I must draw a sword, we probably have bigger problems, sir. But yes, I'm handy with a blade."

"Then take Sim with you, switch clothes and perfect your disguise. Be back here to escort me to the talks at eighth bell. Tommus, you stay here. You and I need a word."

Chapter Twelve

Zan had just ensured that Magram fully understood their instructions by doggedly going over each step three times. The assassin was a formidable force, no doubt, but one with the singularity of purpose akin to an arrow—once loosed, unable to alter its course, even if the situation shifted.

At that moment, a knock on the door interrupted his efforts. A trusted messenger entered, presenting a note on a silver tray, sending their plan into disarray.

"It seems Ghosthand's mage will not be attending today," Zan said. "There was no explanation from Tommus, only an instruction for Genifer Dunn to attend negotiations as normal." Theron nodded in understanding, while Magram gaped in confusion.

Zan and Theron represented Landar's Guildkin, the four families who dominated their nation's commerce. Their leadership resented that Caelon Black, the King's niece, led their delegation. The Guildkin wanted war, yet the infuriating woman was determined to prevent it, promoting the royal agenda over their own.

This was why she had been marked to die at Magram's hand today, along with the Elect. They had spent bells meticulously planning how to make it appear as if Ghosthand's mage had killed them both, and now the woman impersonating Genifer wouldn't even be there.

Zan's plan was to exploit the King's anger over the death of his niece. He was certain this would drive the crown to side with the Guildkin and declare war on a leaderless Mordeland. Despite the plan's brilliance, Jacub Morde seemed to possess more lives than a cat.

"It doesn't change the plan," Theron said, her brow furrowed in thought. "We just need to make it obvious that Morde died at the hand of a mage. Caelon's death will shift blame from us, and none of those present will seem to have magical ability. They certainly won't suspect one of their own. The time for finesse has passed. Just bring this charade of a summit crashing down and then sue for reparations on unreasonable terms. The Elect is responsible for our protection and will be seen to have failed.

She leaned forward slightly, her voice lower but no less certain. "His sister is his successor. She is weak and will struggle to maintain control. She will be easy to manipulate in the aftermath. With Morde gone, the crown will have no choice but to shift its allegiance. The Guildkin will finally take their rightful place in shaping the future."

Zan considered her words. The logic was sound to an extent. He longed for a better plan, but she was right. It was time to act. He glanced at Magram, whose gaze darted between Theron and himself, desperate for simple guidance.

"Don't worry, my friend," Zan said to the killer he had waited decades to unleash on Jacub Morde. "You will do everything we agreed, only this time, you will be inside the room to witness the people responsible for your brother's death meet their end."

Chapter Thirteen

Jacub Morde sat in his chair, listening as Geo skillfully outmanoeuvered the Landar delegate, Caelon Black. Landar had threatened to restrict the shipments of copper and zinc, resources critical to Mordeland's economy. In response, Geo proposed a steep export tariff on grain, a vital commodity that Landar relied upon to supplement their winter stores.

Jacub's heart ached as he watched one of the first women he had ever loved struggle against the Principal Secretary's tactics. The interests of the nation had to come first.

His gaze swept the table as he wondered for the hundredth time who among these people would risk war by assassinating him. So far, Wickham's mysterious mage had kept them at bay, and contract by contract, international tensions were gradually easing.

His left hand strayed to his jacket pocket. He pulled out the note Nalik had written, unfolding it and reading it for the tenth time, fully aware that the man who stood at his shoulder, a flawless imitation of his Master at Arms, would notice him doing so.

Sir, I make no apologies for my actions. Your prejudice leaves you in blind peril. If I must shatter trust in this room to awaken you, so be it. Allow me to continue to protect you from the assassin. Three life-saving reasons to trust me:

Reason One: Yesterday, I saved you from the same assassin who poisoned the gravy. Thwarted by Bernart, he struck out, but I intercepted him. He is deadly and close by. Your time is short.

Reason Two: I'm a stronger healer than a fighter. You must allow a skilled mage to repair the damage to your veins and heart. I'll keep this secret; revealing your illness could weaken your throne. Without intervention, you will die within a few moons.

Reason Three: If your subjects knew you were a charmer, would you and your dynasty survive? I've told no one. I never will. I seek nothing in return for my silence. I was once a charmer myself and understand why you hide it.

Allow me to put my life at risk for the realm. I do not want my children raised under the threat of war.

Jacub felt the tensions rise within him. He stood, walked to the side table, and poured himself a glass of water from the jug beside the vase marked with the yellow flower. Bernart stood nearby, his hands twitching at his sides, the only sign that the Elect serving himself at a formal gathering incensed him.

He's a good man. Loyal as the day is long.

Bernart gave a contained and dignified nod, choosing not to ignore the breach of etiquette entirely.

The silence in the room cut through his thoughts; negotiations had stopped when he left the table. He quickly waved a hand for them to continue. Then he studied Nalik–disguised as Sim–watching the room with unmasked intensity.

Can I trust you?

Earlier, after Nalik had left to change into clothing supplied by Glay, Tommus confirmed he had placed Nalik nearby to foil yesterday's attack. He too made no apologies for his deceit.

Anyone else would be in my dungeons for bringing a mage so close to me. What to do about the man? He has my interests at heart, I'm sure, but he goes too far. In this instance, he seems correct, but I must bring him to heel.

The only mage Jacub trusted had been summoned; permitted to perform an examination, Gil Wickham confirmed Nalik's claim about Jacub's health but admitted his own skills were insufficient to heal him, despite his considerable talent.

Must I trust another mage to heal me? If Nalik wished to skrike me, he could have done so, although the realm would see him punished. A decision to put off until I survive this summit. He dragged his mind back to the discussion.

As if his dark thoughts had summoned demons, the lamplight flickered, and the tall windows on the far wall shattered. The people on either side of the long table were hurled to the floor as if struck by an invisible hand, then pinned in place. Jacub realised the table was sliding his way, rapidly gathering momentum. He stepped back, throwing his arms up in futile defence. His eyes darted around for an escape route or help.

Glay...Nalik staggered back but remained on his feet, flinging out a hand that somehow halted the table's slide inches away from crushing Jacub. Sim was slammed down and forward as if crushed beneath an invisible wall. There was the sickening crack of a bone breaking. The table shook but held its ground.

Chapter Fourteen

Brylee had only a moment to react as she sensed magic flood the room.

Ag's breath, where did this come from?

She had been prepared for an attack, and her plan to shield Jacub Morde with hard air had worked—but the ferocity and sheer power of the assassin's strike caught her off guard. A wedge of hard air hurtled towards the Elect by the water table. Her own counter-wedge deflected it downward into the floor a heartbeat before impact.

The room erupted into chaos before she could track the source of the attack. Windows exploded, showering her with glass shards. Brylee's left hand instinctively rose to protect her face as she jammed her eyes shut. Hot pain seared through her shredded skin as she staggered towards the Elect. Her brow and cheeks were on fire, but the leather buckler she had borrowed from Glay took the brunt of most of the glass slivers.

Her magical sight revealed bodies pinned against walls or the floor, and the table was hurtling towards Jacub Morde. Brylee poured naether into the wedge she had already created, jamming it sideways and anchoring it firmly to the floor. The table slammed into it and shuddered to a stop, vibrating from the force her hidden opponent exerted.

A massive weight slammed down on her from behind, driving her to the floor. Years of sparring with Reni saved her life; instinct kicked in, and she formed two humps of hard air on the floor, twisting her body to land between them. The hard air hammer that pummelled her was foiled by her obstruction, leaving her torso in a small gap beneath it. Her left arm, however, was crushed between the weight and one of the humps—agony blooming until she froze the nerves to her shoulder.

Brylee glanced up and caught her breath. The Elect remained trapped between the wall and the water table, the opposing forces of hard air—hers and the assassin's—made the air shimmer in front of him.

A spear of transparent hard air was forming, pointing directly at the Elect's face. He remained oblivious to the threat. Something about the way the weapon slowly built and readied itself felt deliberate—personal, even—as if the assassin was savouring the moment before striking.

Although she had adjusted her body to dull the pain from her injuries, Brylee was cognisant of the warning signs. Her body was beginning to shut down.

I must be losing too much blood.

She did not have time to assess her injuries. Even maintaining the humps and wedge of air was draining her rapidly. She would pass out in moments if she didn't act.

Brylee hadn't located the assassin, but the idea he might be attacking from outside the room sparked a potential solution. The meeting rooms were on the second floor of the Lord's House. Brylee concentrated on the wooden planks and joists beneath her and the Elect. There wasn't time to burn through them, and transforming them into water would take more time and energy than she had. *Wood fibres. Decomposing them would be too slow.* Then the solution came to her.

Transform them into cork! Similar properties, but much weaker. Brylee visualised what she needed, and years of manipulating the properties of naether did the rest. It took only a second or two for the Elect to fall. His weight, concentrated on a small surface area, sent him plummeting, while hers was spread out enough to keep her stable—at least for now. He dropped like a stone a moment before the air spear slammed into the wall where he had stood.

The floor below Brylee collapsed as she poured more energy into it, and then she was falling. Her eyes were slimy with blood and refused to open. A heartbeat later, she hit a hard surface, surrounded by the sounds of yelling men and smashing plates.

"Get the Elect out of here," Brylee shouted, forgetting to emulate Glay's baritone. Only a second of confusion passed before someone assumed the higher pitch resulted from an injury, then orders were barked. *These are soldiers, good.* She felt herself being lifted by several strong hands and guessed she was also being rushed away.

"The Elect's alive and appears unharmed. Take the Master at Arms directly to Morde's healer." Brylee didn't know who spoke, but it was a voice of command.

"No, take me with the Elect," Brylee said, this time emulating Glay.

"You're a mess, man. You'll bleed out if you don't get help," the voice replied.

"Keep me close to the Elect, or you'll need a healer yourself," Brylee repeated. "By Ag, that's an order." There was no reply, and she felt herself being whisked along, none too gently.

She scanned her surroundings, but there was no trace of magic nearby. That was little comfort, as there had been no such sign earlier when the attack started.

Brylee assessed her body and quickly found a large shard of glass embedded in her neck, draining her lifeblood. Years of experience treating such injuries let her work instinctively. She eased the glass out, enabling a rush of blood through the torn artery. Immediately, she plugged it with air, set about regenerating the damaged tissue as well as and forcing her bones to accelerate blood production. Applying these methods to herself, ones she had refined over her years in hospitals, was sickening but necessary.

Brylee felt the men carrying her stop. The smell of hay and horses reached her. They slid her onto a hard surface that rocked as a carriage door slammed shut. Horses whickered as the driver yelled and showed them his whip and the coach lurched forward. She allowed her mind to rest while her body worked on healing.

It took half a bell to travel to the palace, during which Brylee regenerated some of her lost blood and pushed many of the slivers of glass from her body. She healed most of her superficial wounds, but her arm required more attention. She would need to stand to set it properly before reknitting the bone, mending the ligaments and skin. One-handed, she pulled herself into a sitting position, wiped the drying blood from her eyes, and forced them open.

Two men sat in the carriage with her, and both jumped as she clawed her way upright beside them. Covered in blood, she was a gory sight.

"Lie down, man," said one. "I sent a rider ahead to have the Elect's healer meet us at the palace gate." Brylee shrugged him off.

"It looks a lot worse than it feels," Brylee said. "There's a lot of blood, but mostly scratches. It must be someone else's blood. It's my arm that's the worst of it."

The carriage slowed as they approached the palace, and a short, bearded man in healer's robes climbed in. He hesitated, uncertain where to start. Brylee let him examine her, but she offered no explanation for how there could be so much blood yet so few wounds. The rocking coach made it difficult for him to do much for her arm, aside from offering some pain syrup, which she refused.

A short while later, Brylee was shown into the Elect's private suite, where Jacub and the real Sim Glay were already present. Sim was pouring them both a full glass of wine as she entered. She reached for the door to close it, but the sound of running footsteps in the corridor made her pause. Turning, she saw Tommus, rounding the corner, breathless and red-faced. She stepped inside, and he followed, shutting the door behind him.

"I have an initial report from the Lord's House, sir," Tommus said, catching his breath. The Elect nodded for him to continue.

"Besides the attempt on your life, the worst of it is that Caelon Black is dead. Her neck snapped when she was slammed against the floor with the others. Zan Fallon is furious about the attack on their delegation. He's taken her body, and they are departing for Landar."

Brylee watched Jacub's face slacken at the tragic news. His lips trembled, though he pressed them together. She flinched as the glass in his hand shattered.

"They'll declare war," Jacub said, pushing the others away as they tried to mop the trickle of blood from a cut on his finger.

"Have them detained. Politely. Tell them I'll release them once we've talked. Was anyone else injured?"

He was close to Caelon. Brylee recalled him introducing Caelon to her when she was disguised as Genifer at the opening banquet. *He asked about injuries too quickly, as if to deflect attention from his grief.*

"One of the two men you landed on, sir, has a broken arm and collarbone. He should recover quickly; the Lord's House magical healer is already with him. There are plenty of cuts and bruises among the delegates, but I expected Nalik to be the worst casualty from descriptions of the scene. It was lucky you fell directly into the dining room where the summit's guards were gathered. They claimed Glay... Nalik was in terrible shape."

Brylee listened to his report, clutching her broken arm.

"I got your uniform all bloody, Sim, sorry," she said with a sheepish grin. "But if I can have a healer fix this arm, I think the rest are just scratches." Glay's booming laugh broke the tension in the room.

"If only my body was as resilient as my double's seems to be," he said. "These days, I manage to hurt myself just turning in my sleep."

"What of the assassin?" Jacub said, darkening the moment once more.

"There is absolutely no sign, sir," Tommus replied. "As agreed, no one was allowed in the surrounding corridors or on the floor above. Only the delegates and those Nalik vouched for as being non-magical were permitted. The only guards present were those I had checked by the Council's sensitives, and they were stationed in the Lord's House or on the floor below."

"I didn't have time to locate the attacker, either," Brylee added. "I'd swear there was no mage other than me in the room before the attack. Then suddenly, someone of great power was hurling furniture and smashing windows." She recounted events as she had witnessed them.

"It's just a feeling, sir, but the air spear... it felt personal. I believe whoever this assassin is, they hate you. Personally." The room fell silent for a few moments as everyone digested the events.

"Expending so much magic has left me famished," Brylee said. "I don't know how Sim stands there all day without eating. My stomach rumbled through much of the session."

"Yes, of course," Jacub replied. "And I haven't said it enough. Thank you. I've lost track of how many times you've saved my life. I had my doubts, but–"

"As I said," Brylee replied, cutting off his thought, "I agreed to help because I don't want my daughters to grow up in a country at war. I suppose it's too late now. War seems inevitable."

"Not if we can talk some sense into the Landar representatives," Jacub said.

Chapter Fifteen

Magram recalled the instructions to feign injury and linger with the survivors after killing the Elect and Caelon Black. Jacub Morde and his Master at Arms had escaped, aided by magic, but there had been no sign of the mage responsible.

Had the bloody Trickster been hiding behind the walls? My own ruse turned on me, I suppose. Cunning and smart, that one. She must die as well.

The thought of pursuit had crossed Magram's mind, but the instructions were clear. Under no circumstances reveal your identity. Now that the plan lay in disarray, Magram tightened the magic-restricting knot and hid in plain sight, waiting for the right moment to slip away and seek further instructions from Zan.

While waiting, an unexpected opportunity presented itself. Magram knew showing initiative was frowned upon, as it had gone wrong so many times in the past. Yet this task was crucial. Surely, this time, action would be welcomed.

I know I'm not smart, but this chance might be my last. And it will be beyond the palace walls, aiding my escape.

Nerves gnawed at Magram as doubt crept in. Zan might be angry.

Well, if he is, he can stuff it. I'm the one taking all the risks. If he objects, I'll kill him myself and hunt the monster, Jacub, alone. At least I killed Caelon.

Brother, vengeance begins at last.

It felt good to act. It silenced the fear and worry, replacing them with purpose.

Magram looked in the mirror; clothes and hair needed straightening. Dishevelled, but good enough for one final, desperate strike.

One of us dies today, Jacub. And if I see Trickster, her ashes will mingle with yours.

Chapter Sixteen

The Landar delegation had been diverted to the harbour Customs House but not without incident. A minor skirmish had resulted in one death and several injuries. Jacub decided it would be a grand gesture for him to travel there rather than have the delegation dragged back to the palace. However, even with everyone rushing their tasks, little happened quickly when it came to the Elect's travel arrangements.

Twenty mounted guards and two carriages had to be prepared, one for the Elect and his small party, the other for his Principal Secretary's entourage. In addition, Brylee and Wickham had persuaded Tommus, who in turn convinced the Elect, to include mages in the party. Given the circumstances, Jacub did not argue.

He sent word to the Council of Magical Law to provide two mages skilled in combat. Brylee, disguised as Sim Glay, and Wickham would remain close to the Elect while the two other mages would ride ahead as scouts and behind as a rear guard.

While everything was being prepared, the Elect went to change and freshen up. Brylee had Wickham pretend to heal her arm while she discreetly did it herself. She spent time in front of a mirror, ensuring her face and arms bore the small injuries consistent with shattered glass and her fall through the floor.

"I'm going to check in with my investigators," Tommus said, walking out the door. He called back over his shoulder, "Don't wait for me. I'll catch up with you at the Customs House." As he made his way towards his office, Genifer Dunn rounded the corner in front of him. She looked shaken but didn't appear to have any serious injuries.

"How are you doing, my dear?" Tommus said, stopping and placing a hand on her shoulder.

"I'll survive, but it's doubtful Geo Kant will. I've come in her place. I was with her and the healers when the Elect's messenger summoned her to the Customs House. She seemed fine at first but fainted upon hearing the news. The healer thinks she is bleeding in her brain and is monitoring her closely. How is Jacub?"

"The Elect is fine, and will be glad of your counsel, I'm sure. Go, I'll catch up with you in due course."

A man and a woman waited in his office. Edi Ko, the senior maid of the household staff, was also the head of Tommus's palace spy network. He had relied on her for a decade. Almost nothing transpired in the palace without her knowledge. Neil Linpine, the palace guard's chief investigator, reported jointly to Sim and Tommus.

Tommus heard their initial reports, which provided little useful information. He decided to take a broader approach.

"Let's go back to the beginning. Step through every event from the past few days carefully. I know in my heart we've missed something."

Starting from the first report that there could be an attempt on the Elect's life during the summit, they painstakingly listed each snippet of information and pieced them together into a comprehensive timeline. It added a lot of detail, but provided little useful knowledge. Tommus's mind raced. He was supposed to be the Ghosthand, yet it seemed the assassin could spirit himself in and out of their midst unseen, like a phantom. The thought of ghosts reminded him of Brylee's suggestion.

"Did you question everyone near the chapel incident to see if they noticed anything quirky or out of place?" Tommus asked.

"I got nothing but strange looks for my questions," Neil replied.

"Same here," Edi said. "Oh, Lannis the gardener bent my ear, of course. He's always got a tale to tell. Went on about apples for ages. It's just an old man's waffling, it is."

"Tell me anyway, but keep it short," Tommus said.

"Well, you wouldn't guess it but his eyes are failing. They are fine for close-up work, such as inspecting plants, but he can't see more than four paces. I'm already looking for a replacement. Anyway, the point is, he recognises people at a distance by their scent. Apparently, I smell of lilies, the Elect of fine wine, and so on."

"What do I smell of?" Tommus asked, rolling his eyes and glancing at the candle to see how much time had elapsed.

"I'd rather not say, sir. But one of the Privy Council members cut through the chapel gardens while Lannis was tending the sickleroot. They hurried, but they were too late. Lannis had heard the big wooden door close and Loral's voice murmuring through the walls. Ag keep him safe.

Lannis said he didn't know who it was at first, as they didn't smell familiar. But when they got close enough, he could see them clearly. He said they didn't smell of apples, like they should. He was quite agitated about it. When he heard about the deaths, he took it as an omen."

Tommus's breath caught in his chest. "Which Privy Council member did he see?" he asked, recalling that all the members were present inside the chapel throughout the ceremony.

Edi told them the name and explained how sure Lannis was because up close he could see their distinctive birthmark, before the Master of the Seal leapt from his seat and fled the room.

Chapter Seventeen

The Elect, Genifer Dunn, and Sim Glay rode in the first carriage. There was a brief attempt at discussing how best to calm the Landar delegation, but the conversation dwindled soon after they passed through the palace gates.

At first, Jacub's head swivelled constantly, scanning for danger, but eventually, he seemed to calm himself, sitting back with his eyes closed. Though his body remained rigid and alert rather than sleepy, his expression revealed a mind racing through details. Sim sat alone on his side of the carriage, his back to the horses. Every few moments, he moved to the opposite window, anxiously watching the crowd.

The second carriage followed, carrying four of Geo Kant's staff, all greatly upset by her injury. Genifer ignored them, suggesting instead she travel in Jacub's carriage where she could be more useful. The Elect had cautioned her that the assassin might strike again and she would be safer travelling separately, but she had put on a determined expression and insisted on being where he needed her the most.

Two dozen mounted guards kept pace, split into three units of eight. Each unit was composed of a mix of fresh fighters and summit guards, injured or not, in case they spotted anything that might identify the assassin who had been in their midst. Each was led by a mage: a tall, rangy woman in mage's robes led the vanguard, while a rotund mage who could barely stay in the saddle commanded the rear guard.

Wickham rode with the soldiers between the two carriages. Two survivors of the meeting room flanked him. One, his head and face covered in bandages, while the other had a heavily bound leg. Unable to dismount, he carried a crossbow, ready to fire from the saddle.

Wickham sweated with concentration as he maintained a shield of hard air around the Elect's coach while they cantered through Nuulan's streets. Anchoring it to the carriage provided some stability, but the jostling motion of his horse and the coach made it nearly impossible to sustain its integrity. It was better than nothing; perhaps it would deflect a first thrust from the enemy.

Magram took all of this in as the procession reached Cutler's Market. There, the busy evening traffic offered the perfect opportunity to escape after striking. Uncovering Jacub's magical defences had been effortless; a few questions had revealed everything. Magram's only disappointment was that there was no sign of the Trickster.

Careful now. We know what she looked like asleep next to Genifer, but she hid from us cleverly last time. A fractional loosening of the knot brought more clarity to Magram's magical sight. Even so, the scan around the carriage revealed nothing threatening. Even the magical abilities of the three mages Jacub had identified weren't visible to someone with such limited magical perception.

As she lamented her inability, she began to relish the sweet taste of revenge. Morde would pay for his evil acts with a painful death, right here in the carriage. She would find an excuse to stop the procession, step out, and let it roll on with his corpse and that of his Master at Arms.

She loosened what she called her knot of deceit a little more. A dark thrill coursed through her as she stalked her prey, eyes locking onto Sim Glay. She would knock him out first before killing him. He had always been kind to Genifer, unlike the monster Morde, and didn't need to suffer. Perhaps she would let him live, she mused.

"It's time for you to pay, Jacub," she said, placing her hand on his knee. A surge of power filled her as she invaded his personal space. She enjoyed the moment of confusion on the Elect's face as she slammed Glay's head back into the carriage wall. The unexpected blow required little force. His eyes rolled back in his head as she turned her attention to her prey.

She tugged on her knot and let it unravel completely. Power flooded into her, filling her with euphoria, as though she had expanded to fill the entire carriage and beyond.

Magram clutched the Elect's knee tighter as he pulled away, squirming to escape towards the corner. She erected a barrier around them to contain him and keep his squealing from alerting the guards. As she studied him, intent on savouring his realisation of his impending death, she noticed he, too, was brimming with magic. The moment her hand gripped his knee her magical sight had come alive, revealing a man of power at her side. Initially, she had missed it, too focused on neutralising Glay.

The fleeting amount of surprise on the Elect's face saved Magram's life. The delay allowed her to realise all was not as it seemed and fling a hastily crafted shield around herself. Heavy blows rained down upon it, driving her back several inches. The Elect's jaw was set, his facial muscles taut as he braced himself against the board at his back.

If you want to test your power against mine, I welcome it, thought Magram, drawing in as much magic as she could. She anchored it to the sidewall and hurled a crushing force at the Elect with all her might. He threw up his arms, resisting, but he was already shrinking back, his feeble shield wavering under the pressure. Magram reinforced her own protection and bore down.

"Genifer and I have planned this for decades, you monster," Magram growled, straining with effort. This should have been over by now and she couldn't imagine how he was resisting.

It's the Trickster, her mind screamed. Agony raked across Magram's face; a heat so intense she nearly abandoned her magic to claw at it with her bare hands. She had never faced a victim who fought back. Her attacks were never fights; they were single death blows. She had the presence of mind to use her magic to douse her face, quelling the fire instantly. Clamping her eyes closed, she began to bludgeon the Trickster with everything she had.

Each thrust was devastating, sending waves of searing heat—the same heat she had once used to incinerate Ghosthand's dog above the courtyard privy.

Chapter Eighteen

It happened in a heartbeat. Brylee spun around as Genifer Dunn's seemingly non-magical link surged violently, expanding into a grotesquely bloated pipe. Magic flooded the carriage. Through her magical sight, Brylee watched in awe as Genifer tugged at a complex knot at the juncture of her link to the world's flow of naether. Brylee had never imagined such a feat, yet she instinctively grasped its purpose. She braced herself as Sim Glay's head snapped back, and he slumped down on the plush bench seat.

Brylee reinforced the shield she had conjured the moment she entered the carriage, a precaution she had taken after persuading the Elect to let her take his place on the journey. She stabbed with an invisible spear of air, but it bounced off as her attacker's own barrier suddenly flared to life.

A crushing pressure slammed her backwards; she could barely breathe. She knew at once she couldn't pierce a magical wall forged by someone so powerful, so she changed tactics. She heated the air near the assassin's face, bringing a momentary reprieve.

The cabin rocked violently as wave after wave of power rained down on her like a blacksmith's hammer. She had only moments to react before darkness swallowed her, yet could think of no way to retaliate.

Brylee had one thought: escape. She couldn't win in such a confined space, and Sim's unconscious body was being repeatedly flung around by Genifer's relentless attacks. She broadened her magical sight, analysing the carriage's construction. Dovetailed joints, glued and nailed, bound the structure. She redirected her heat energy into the joints, and within seconds, the wall behind her collapsed. As she fell backwards, Genifer's next strike propelled her head over heels into the street, sending her crashing into a market stall filled with bolts of cloth. Her shield and the soft landing saved her from serious injury.

The carriage skidded sideways as its horses reared to a stop and the wooden wheels struck the low curb. The coach flipped onto its side, toppling through market stalls, sending people scrambling for safety.

"Protect the Elect," she heard a man call, likely Wickham. The cry was quickly taken up by others. Men leapt from their horses to aid Brylee, unaware that she was a decoy. She looked up at the real Jacub Morde, astride his horse next to Wickham, his face bandaged to conceal his identity.

Even with his face wrapped in cloth, Brylee could see the indecision on his face. They had agreed he would flee in an ambush, yet he clearly didn't want to leave her to her fate. Brylee hid her face with her arm and made a slight adjustment to her features, so she still resembled Mordeland's leader, but it was a little off. She hauled herself to her feet and pointed at Jacub.

"That's the real Elect," Brylee yelled. "To him! I'm a decoy." She barely had time to take in the sea of confused faces before instinct jerked her attention towards the toppled carriage. Genifer's dress was torn, her face bloodied. Whatever her injuries, they weren't slowing her down. A lance of heat shot from her as she hauled herself out of the wreckage. Brylee dove to the side, feeling a scorching rush as the cloth bolts she had scattered erupted in flames.

"Dunn is the assassin!" Wickham yelled from his horse, which he had nudged in front of the Elect's as he erected a protective shield. "Ride, sir. Your presence only ties her hands." The Elect glared at him, then realised he was right. Jacub snatched the bandages from his face.

"This unit with me," he yelled, pointing at the rear guard. "The rest of you help Nalik kill the assassin." He dug his heels into his mount's flanks, wheeling around and galloping through the ranks.

Beside Genifer, a cart filled with vegetables rose into the air and hurtled towards Brylee and the encircling guards. Brylee reached out with a blocking force, staggering backwards as the wagon crashed down mere feet away. She was no match for such power.

Arrows filled the air, streaking away from the six archers among the remaining guards. They bounced harmlessly off Genifer's shield. One bolt slammed into the carriage beneath Genifer, striking a nerve. She glowered at the man who had fired it. Moments later, he screamed as he burst into flames.

I need to take this somewhere else, thought Brylee. She scanned for the nearest building. It was two stories tall with a brown stone façade and a flat roof, typical of Nuulan. She sprinted towards it, conjuring steps of hard air in front of her as she went. Bounding up them, it appeared to those in the market that she was running through the air.

To their credit, several guards fumbled for the steps, attempting to keep up. She dissolved the stairs behind her to prevent them following, then turned to find the assassin.

Genifer threw her head back and roared, before setting off in Brylee's wake. She didn't bother with hard air stairs. Instead, she ascended on a moving column of air, gliding over the market stalls, arrow shafts snapping inches from her skin.

Brylee had barely taken a few strides across the roof when a tree-thick lance of air flew past her head. She dove and rolled behind a chimney stack, fully aware it only provided a brief reprieve. Pressing her back into it to catch her breath, she was suddenly thrown forward as the chimney exploded and the bricks toppled around her. Her shield was the only thing saving her from being crushed by falling masonry.

She glanced back as she ran. Genifer was marching towards her, her face set in grim determination, and her eyes burning with anger.

Fleeing towards the next chimney, Brylee ripped roof tiles beneath her pursuer, flinging them at Genifer's shield. The assassin's footing wavered briefly, but she righted herself with hard air, levitating two feet above the roof as she advanced, relentless.

A rock-hard wall of air materialised in Brylee's path. She slammed her foot down, arresting her momentum as she threw up her arms, but her head still collided with the rippling surface.

Invisible forces grabbed her, yanking her off the ground and spinning her around. She wove protection around herself, keeping the worst of the crushing pressure at bay, but her energy was draining fast.

Genifer stomped through the debris, halting a dozen strides away. Panting, she planted her feet, immense strain cording her neck muscles and distorting her face into a demonic grimace.

Brylee had little left beyond her magical sight. Every ounce of her being fought against the forces relentlessly crushing her. She looked on helplessly as an unfamiliar weave of magic swirled around her foe, enclosing her in a cocoon.

Brylee redoubled her efforts, knowing her fate if she didn't break through. She cried out as her body absorbed some of the attack's force while she diverted a fraction of her magic from defence to offence.

Levi had trained her in mental attacks, and she had honed a technique to sever an opponent's anchor point for hard air manipulation. She reached out, attempting to alter Genifer's bones and her organs, but each tactic failed to penetrate the strange weave.

Genifer was suddenly rocked on her feet, her head snapping around. Somehow, Wickham had lifted himself onto the roof and magically torn a stone gargoyle from its mount. He had lifted it high and hurled it down onto the assassin's back.

Genifer's weave buckled but held, and with a flick of her arm, she sent Wickham flying end over end, backwards over the roof's edge into the market below. Brylee cried out after him, her heart breaking.

"Why are you doing this, Genifer?" Brylee cried, as she channelled the last of her energy to shore up her defence. She felt the pressure ease slightly, but she was trapped as soundly as if a stone giant had clasped her in its hands.

"My name is Magram," her attacker growled.

"Yet you look like Genifer."

"As did you, Trickster. I should have killed you while you slept next to my sister."

"You are Genifer's twin? This isn't about trade wars for you, is it? It's personal." Brylee was clutching at straws, attempting to keep the woman talking until help arrived or she could think of something.

"A twin now, but we were triplets once," Magram said. The fire in her expression dimmed as she sifted through old memories. "Dendry was our brother, killed by the monster you protect."

Brylee coughed as the pressure crashed down on her again.

"I didn't... know! Tell me about Dendry!"

"He's dead. And I loved him. That's all you need to know."

"I loved my own brother. My heart broke when he was crushed by a cart." Brylee had to keep her talking.

"Tricking me into delaying won't help. I'll just kill more of the monster's men."

"Then explain! Convince me! I don't believe Morde's a monster."

Magram's expression faltered, then twisted again as the pressure on Brylee intensified.

"I was smart back then. Smarter than Genifer. But Morde left me injured and rode away. He abandoned me. Genifer says that if he had taken me to a healer, I might have recovered. My brain might have worked properly once more. Instead, he killed Dendry and left me to rot." Brylee felt the pressure notch up another degree. "Why are you spoiling our plan? Why are you protecting him?"

"I don't really know him," Brylee grunted as she began to run out of air. "I only met him a day ago. It was more about averting a war than protecting the Elect. Are you certain about him? If you send me to Ag, and I see my brother, I need to be able to tell him why you killed me."

"With you gone, the monster won't be far behind you. You can ask him yourself. Or ask her—I already snapped her neck."

"I don't–" Brylee's vision was going grey. "Who? This makes no sense. You've missed something." Brylee couldn't focus on Magram's face but felt her grip falter. *Am I getting through?*

"No! I get things wrong, but Genifer knows. She said I'm right. Caelon and Jacub are filthy, evil killers."

"I'm sure she's right. She seemed intelligent. Help me understand." Brylee knew she had to buy time, but forming the words of betrayal still galled her. "If I understood, perhaps I'd help you kill him. Has he tricked me, too?"

Aside from her blood pounding in her head, there was silence, but Brylee had lost all sense of time. After what felt like a lifetime, the pressure eased a fraction, and she gulped down a breath.

"I'll tell you quickly. Then I'll kill you dead. Then I'll hunt the monster."

Chapter Nineteen

Thirty-two years earlier, Rynta in Eastern-Landar

"Don't go, Dendry," Magram said, a note of desperation in her tone. She held him by the shoulder as he tried to push past her. She considered using magic on him, but he would have hated it. He had his own power, and they had agreed never to use it on each other since their childhood bickering had left her with burnt hair and him with a scar across his brow.

"I'm going. Get out of my way."

"If Genifer were here, she would take my side." Their sister, just minutes older, worked as a scribe for the Landarian delegation. Jacub Morde, heir to the Morde Dynasty, was visiting in place of his father, who was getting too old for long sea voyages.

"I've spent a year courting Caelon and was making progress. Now she's only got eyes for the young princeling."

"They don't call them kings and princes in Mordeland, Dendry. Besides, you're the son of the stablemaster. Caelon is your lord's daughter, and he is brother to the king. When the current king passes, her father ascends, and one day, she might be queen. Get your head out of your breeches and the clouds. She's nice to you because she believes you are the best riding teacher, and she wants to win the tourney next year."

"She's only being nice to him because she's always talking about going to our King's Court. She's hoping some of his airs will rub off on her."

"What's wrong with that?"

"I saw the way he looked at her on the hunt. He wants to rub off on her, all right. They're riding down to the old, flooded quarry on a moonlit night."

"What do you plan to do about it? You're not even stablemaster yet."

"I don't know. I'll hide in the bushes and use magic to make him spill wine on her or something. She'll think him a buffoon." He broke her grip on his shoulder, strode to the door, flung it open, and marched out.

If you're going, you idiot, so am I, Magram thought.

Her brother had left his horse saddled after his day's duties. By the time she ran to the stables, he was mounted. He kicked Sarag's flanks and galloped off into the darkness.

Magram ran to Lelly's stall. She grabbed a bridle, quickly fitted the bit into the mare's mouth, and yanked the straps tight. There was no time for a saddle. She led her pony to a mounting block and leapt on, bareback.

The wind grabbed at her as she cantered down the bridleway towards the old quarry. In the distance, she could hear the celebrations echoing from the open windows at the Lord's House, fading behind her.

She slowed as she approached the final row of trees at the summit's ridge above the quarry. Sarag was tethered to a pine, grazing on bondleberries from a bush at his feet. Magram tied Lelly's reins to the same tree and crept forward.

Between her and the lake lay a small copse of bushes. Beyond, she spotted two fettered horses near a pair of silhouettes. The water was still, and the moon's reflection glistened on its surface, mirroring the trees on the far shore.

She heard a woman's laugh as she advanced in a crouch, using the bushes for cover. She found Dendry skulking within their shadows, his aura so bright that even a non-magical person might have spotted it on a darker night. He startled, having not heard her approach, when she tugged on his sleeve.

"Let's go. You can't do any good here." He jerked away from her and glared across the clearing. "What do you think she'll make of you spying on her? Do you think she'll thank you for embarrassing her in front of the future leader of Mordeland?"

For a moment, Magram thought her words were reaching him, but when he stiffened, she followed his gaze and saw Jacub leaning in and kissing Caelon on the mouth. It was too much for Dendry. Before she could react, he was running through the dark.

Jacub heard him approach, not a hard feat as Dendry shouted incoherently, and pulled himself to his feet.

"What's wrong?" Jacub began, but Dendry's awkwardly thrown right hook sent him sprawling on his back.

"Dendry, what on earth?" Caelon yelled, leaping up and pummelling his chest with her fists. Dendry gave her an intense, cold stare, his teeth clenched. Even from her hiding spot, Magram could feel his sense of betrayal radiating from him.

Jacub rolled onto his front, pushed to his knees, and stood. His face was flushed as blood trickled from the corner of his mouth. He stepped forward and punched Dendry. This was no awkward fist of a stable hand, but the product of years of training in the bailey under the Master at Arms. By design, the blow started from Jacub's feet, driving up through his hips and into his pivoting shoulders, unleashing all the power his embarrassed rage produced. It connected with Dendry's jaw, knocking him to the ground.

Magram watched it all unfold from her hiding place behind the treeline. She heard Morde yelling at Caelon to get on her horse, but the woman argued that they couldn't just leave the boy there. She later recalled being annoyed at the term boy. Her brother had seen eighteen summers and ran the stables when their father was away. Morde convinced Caelon to ride with him by insisting it wasn't safe. What if Dendry had friends nearby? He promised to send men to help the stablemaster's son when they reached her father's house.

As Jacub and Caelon mounted, Magram reached out with her magic to her brother. It was hard to tell at this distance, but he didn't appear to be breathing. She ran out of the bushes to help Dendry, just as Jacub galloped past on one of his father's stallions. It barrelled right into her, knocking her to the ground.

She woke in the stable yard with the vet tending to the bump on her head. They told her that Dendry was dead, and Jacub claimed he had not seen her as he rode away. Caelon supported his story.

It didn't make sense to Magram, but nothing had since her brother's death. No matter how hard she tried, her mind no longer worked as it once had.

And something else had changed. She and Dendry had always been gifted with generous links to the magical source, but since his death, hers had doubled. The estate's mage found it unusual for someone to inherit another's link while unconscious, but not unheard of.

It was the biggest 'gift' she had ever received in her life; all the ones she skriked later were far smaller.

Chapter Twenty

Present day

Magram held off crushing her prisoner while she told her story. At different points in the tale, she'd felt a whirlwind of emotions: sadness, fear, and shock, all raw and visceral. But overshadowing them all, the one that lingered the longest, was the humiliation of being trampled by those of noble birth, and her disgust at how they closed ranks to protect their own.

The Trickster did not seem like them, despite looking like Morde, but she would skrike the Trickster's power as well and make it her own.

"You fought well, Trickster," Magram said. "I'll tell the Elect you did when I crush his skull."

Magram steadied herself. She knew she was cunning, but not clever. She could not afford to make a mistake. She needed a plan. She thought through how she would squeeze the life from the Trickster until he fainted, then skrike him.

Yes, that would do it.

Magram reached for her full power, knowing she'd need every drop to destroy her nemesis—and to keep full control. But instead of surging, her magic dwindled to almost nothing. Alarmed, she turned her magical sight to her link's knot, only to find it drawn so tight she had less power than some charmers she'd met. Somehow, the Trickster had found her knot—and pulled it tight.

There was no time to react. A white-hot spear of hard air ploughed through her brain, and everything went black.

Chapter Twenty-One

Bernart eyed her mask with what Brylee could only describe as suspicious dignity. His demeanour was deferential, almost obsequious, and she suspected Jacub had told him that the grossly disfigured woman in front of him was somehow a part of Tommus's group—the very ones who had saved the Elect a week earlier. He stepped back and allowed her to enter Jacub's bed chamber.

Earlier that morning, she had walked through the scene of her battle with Magram on the way to the palace. The building where Wickham and Tommus had found her battered body stood derelict, its upper levels now covered in canvas.

Rumours among the suspicious city folk ensured that repairs would be stalled for many moons; people were certain that lingering magic released there might corrupt anyone who approached, risking turning them into a charmer.

In stark contrast, the market was thriving.

News of the battle had spread, capturing the imagination of bards, storytellers, and merchants eager to profit from tales of the 'Battle of the Bizarre' and 'The Elect's Arcane Shield.' The square's inn was now named The Enchanted Guardian.

Brylee had shaken her head in dismay at how the damaged goods now sold for grossly inflated prices. The same people who feared the cursed building had no qualms about hawking the broken wares for profit.

Wickham had tears in his eyes when Brylee finally woke and spoke his name. He explained how he had barely managed to keep her alive, using what medical knowledge he had to prevent her from slipping away. Twice, he thought he had lost her until more experienced healers arrived.

The damage to her body was extensive, but what concerned him most was her brain. He feared it might be permanent damage.

While Brylee slept, Wickham had summoned one of the most talented magical healers he could find to repair what she could of Brylee's limbs and damaged organs. She hadn't known what to make of Brylee's face, which, to Wickham, appeared to have been trapped midway through one of her transformations. Her patient had a man's body, but some puzzlingly feminine traits remained.

In the end, Wickham directed the healer to do only enough to ensure Brylee's survival, leaving the finer work to Brylee herself, knowing her abilities far surpassed anyone unfamiliar with her unique magic.

Once awake, it had taken Brylee several days to stabilise her body and heal the worst of her injuries. Still in shock and drained, she lacked the strength to perform the more nuanced arts required to restore herself to normal.

Today, her body still resembled the Elect's, though she moved like a man twice his age. The mask she wore concealed a face so scarred even she couldn't bear to see in the mirror, a sight she wouldn't wish upon anyone else.

She accepted the warm cup of tea Bernart offered and eyed the chocolate-covered biscuits resting on the plate on the small table by her chair.

"If that's everything, sir," he said to Jacub, who lay propped up on silk pillows on his large four-poster bed.

"Yes. Ensure we are not disturbed," Jacub replied. As the dapper man withdrew, Brylee heard him whisper to Sim Glay, who had stationed himself outside the Elect's bedroom door. Neither he nor Bernart knew who the masked stranger was, and they were clearly uneasy about leaving him with their master. The door clicked shut, and Brylee turned her attention to her patient.

"Lie back and relax, sir. Keep very still," she said. "There will be no pain, but your body will feel strange." She reached out with her mind, more cautiously than she might have if she were fully recovered—and her patient wasn't the nation's ruler. Slowly, she began locating and transforming his pockets of fatty tissue in his arteries into blood. Although delicate, clearing blood vessels took far less magic than healing herself.

"Transforming the bad tissue is fairly straightforward," Brylee explained. "What we need to be careful of is how your body reacts to suddenly having significantly better blood flow. Your blood pressure will change within your system and might expose secondary issues, which I need to find and fix as we go.

"You might feel euphoric as more air gets to your brain. Perhaps lightheaded. I need to go slowly and do several treatments over the next three days. I doubt you'll accept bedrest—you'll feel amazing—but please take things easy."

"Are you sure you won't consider a permanent role at court, Nalik?" Jacub said. Brylee dismissed the offer, but his use of her fake name gave her pause.

"Nalik was my brother. I don't know why I used his name when you caught me off guard. I'm clearly not cut out for spying. I'm Brylee. But I'll take a pass on the offer. I have a life to get back to. Is war inevitable?" Jacub smiled and shook his head, earning a sharp admonishment for moving.

"I doubt it. There is less chance of it than there was two weeks ago. Nydros and the Thraevens have agreed to honour the decisions reached before the attack. Genifer, Zan, and Theron are under arrest, sequestered in the Lord's House. Geo, who is feeling much better, sailed yesterday to return Caelon's body to her father, the King, carrying a letter from me outlining the actions of his Guildkin."

"What do you expect he will do?" Brylee took a biscuit and, protocol be damned, dunked it in her tea before swallowing it whole.

"I think we found sufficient evidence to support our claims, and both Nydros and Thraeven have submitted written testimony to corroborate them. Publicly, they are supporting our version of events. This will place the king in a bind, as the Guildkin's support is foundational to his throne and national stability. However, I suspect they will all want to sweep this under the rug."

Jacub sighed and added, "On a personal level, though, the King will demand justice for his daughter's death. He'll want the prisoners back for trial and execution. We'll have to address that in due course."

Brylee paused her work as she sensed Jacub's body tense, likely reacting to the memories of his youth with Caelon. She hadn't shared Magram's accusations with anyone and had no idea if Genifer had confessed her motives.

Brylee wanted to ask what it was like to discover someone who had worked so closely with him for almost thirty summers had been plotting his death, but decided to let the matter rest. Instead, she helped herself to a second biscuit and asked a different, challenging question.

"May I ask you a personal question, sire?"

He looked cautious but said nothing. Brylee decided to take his lack of refusal as consent.

"Your reputation paints you as fair, but ruthless—and if you'll forgive me—a little arrogant. And Magram told me why she hated you: Dendry." The Elect's expression clouded, but she pressed on.

"I'm sure she's twisted events in her mind, but her story paints a picture of someone heartless, uncaring, and selfish. Yet that isn't the man lying here in front of me. The man loved by those closest to him. The man who garners the respect of people like Tommus and Bernart. The man who knows the names of his guards and cares about their well-being. Was Magram completely wrong?"

Jacub shifted uncomfortably, his face flushing as he wrapped his arms across his chest. He didn't speak for a long time, and Brylee began to think he had no intention of answering. She wished she had kept her mouth shut.

"No, I think she was close enough," the Elect said at last. He didn't meet Brylee's eyes, keeping his gaze fixed on the ornate ceiling.

"Obviously, I hit back out of reflex—anger, embarrassment. I don't think I even realised he was dead until they told me. I don't recall seeing the girl at all. I was so young. But none of that is an excuse. I did those things.

"Worse, I let my father and uncle cover it all up. People were paid off or sent abroad, and I was whisked back to Mordeland soon after. No one would speak to me about it. I was ashamed, believe me. But I didn't pursue it as I should have. It didn't take long for me to accept what they told me—that there was no sense in digging up the past, as it would change nothing."

"But that isn't where you left it, is it?"

"No. I was arrogant and spoilt. Those events made me believe I was untouchable. And then I wasn't. There was another moment, in my early twenties—when I made a decision that cost lives, when someone I loved died because of my choices—when I understood that power doesn't absolve you. It only means your mistakes carry a heavier cost.

"The shame from that experience set off a chain reaction, one that led back to Dendry. It made me question the man I'd become— and the man I wanted to be. And when my father's health began to fail, I had to ask myself who the country needed me to be."

"What did you do?"

"Ultimately, I grew up. The maturity I lacked finally caught up with me. Being surrounded by good men like Sim Glay rubbed off on me. And when I heard Genifer had entered service, I cleared some roadblocks for her. But don't get me wrong—she earned her position every day."

"Did you ever talk to her about it?"

"I tried. Once. She accepted my apology too easily. I put that down to my position. Now I know what she and her twin were plotting, I see it all in a different light. Shamed again, and... a little foolish. And once more, people have died because of my actions and inactions."

He fell silent, lost in thought, and Brylee left him to it, focusing instead on the main artery to his heart.

"Will you restart the trade talks?" she asked, resuming her work once enough time had passed.

"I think they've served their purpose. While Landar resolves its issues, our ambassadors have work to do securing last week's concessions. I suspect the Guildkin won't be pleased things are progressing without them and will demand a seat at the table. Geo's trip to Landar will be her last official act as Principal Secretary. The head of the Trilogy rotates with the next moon, and the new chair will approach me with a different agenda, I'm sure."

"Yebba Bane?" Brylee said, glad of the mask hiding the grin she couldn't suppress.

"Yes, she's quite a handful, as you can imagine."

"And a mage. That's interesting." Brylee was full of questions but pressed her lips together to contain them.

"Quite," Jacub replied after a pause. "Tommus confided that she realised you were not the real Genifer when she saw your magic." Brylee wasn't surprised. Reflecting on recent events, she had wondered about the strange glances the woman had given her and realised Jacub must have been worried about Yebba realising he was a charmer as well.

Best not to touch that. They need to work that out themselves.

"You were never considering approving her plan for a military navy, were you?" she asked instead.

"Are you sure you don't want a role at court, Brylee? You are quite perceptive. No, Geo had already negotiated that we would use the Nydros privateer fleet. Her proposal was just a ruse to put pressure on the Thraevens."

"There," Brylee said, taking her last sip of tea and putting her cup down next to the empty biscuit plate. "I've finished for today, but lie still for a few minutes, and move slowly for the next two bells. Avoid meetings with Yebba, or anyone who will raise your blood pressure."

"Thank you, Brylee. I mean that. The throne owes you a boon. What can I do for you?" he asked. Brylee thought about it.

"Nothing, sir," she replied. "Respect my wish to return to my life, with my anonymity intact. It feels trite to say, but I acted for the good of the nation. However, I would appreciate it if you could use your position to improve the lot of us charmers. The stigma is unjustified and cruel. I appreciate why you can't just make a proclamation, but I'm sure you would if it were that simple."

"Yes, it's the work of generations. I'll ensure it progresses as quickly as these things can. Working closely with Yebba will no doubt keep that sentiment in the forefront of my mind for the next twelve moons." As Brylee stood, Jacub extended his hand to shake hers. "Are you sure there's nothing else?"

"Well, I do have an interest in the Wispy Weed business. Wickham's mission pulled me away from assisting in the trade talks with Nydros. I'm not asking for special treatment, but I would like to ensure I haven't lost out on what I would have negotiated..."

What's Next?

Thank you for reading *Webs of Treason*, a *Weavers of Destiny* novella. I hope you loved the journey as much as I loved writing it.

Enjoyed the Book?

Please consider leaving a review—even just a few lines—on Amazon, Goodreads, or your preferred platform. Reviews help other readers discover stories they'll love, and they mean the world to authors.

Read the Complete Duology

If you haven't already, the *Weavers of Destiny* duology is complete and ready for you to explore—or revisit here:
www.andrewplatten.com/books/

Book One: *Strands of Time and Magic*
Book Two: *Chains of Fear and Fury*

Get a Free Novella

Sign up for my newsletter at www.andrewplatten.com and receive *Bonds of Ascension* for free. This novella explores Lu's coming of age in the fierce Mobi'dern clan, set before the events of *Strands of Time and Magic*.

Stay Connected

Visit www.andrewplatten.com to sign up for early access to stories, behind-the-scenes extras, and exclusive offers.

Acknowledgements

Heartfelt thanks to Andrew Tsui, Mike Hrycyk, and Darren Bold for your thoughtful feedback and insights as alpha readers—your input helped shape this story in ways I couldn't have done alone. And to Darielle, who is so much more than an alpha reader: thank you for your unwavering support, sharp editorial eye, and for walking this journey with me every step of the way.

About the Author

Born in England, I emigrated to Canada with my two children and now live in the Comox Valley on Vancouver Island.

My initial career was in technology; a realm akin to magic with its ability to make lives better (and worse). It has mystery, a language few can master, and often fails us just when we need it most. It's no surprise to me that many who revel in fantasy are drawn from the ranks of technology.

I am a view junkie and am drawn to places where I can imagine being an explorer discovering them for the first time. It's why I became a pilot. People-watching is also one of my favourite hobbies. I try to understand how our minds, perceptions, and emotions work. The hundreds of hours of podcasts and papers I devour don't make me a psychology expert, but they have helped me develop the characters that act out the book's plot.

Oh, and I am tormented by cheese. I love cheese.

Learn more about me, my work, events, and bonus content at www.andrewplatten.com

www.ingramcontent.com/pod-product-compliance
Lightning Source LLC
Chambersburg PA
CBHW020311150626
46552CB00022B/2767